Club Luxe

Book 5: New Beginnings

ISBN-13: 978-1511670296
ISBN-10: 1511670290
Copyright © 2014 Olivia Noble
All rights reserved.

Table of Contents

CHAPTER ONE	1
CHAPTER TWO	7
CHAPTER THREE	18
CHAPTER FOUR	28
CHAPTER FIVE	38
CHAPTER SIX	45
CHAPTER SEVEN	54
CHAPTER EIGHT	65
CHAPTER NINE	76
CHAPTER TEN	86
CHAPTER ELEVEN	96
CHAPTER TWELVE	103
CHAPTER THIRTEEN	110
CHAPTER FOURTEEN	119
CHAPTER FIFTEEN	127
CHAPTER SIXTEEN	136
CHAPTER SEVENTEEN	142

Billionaires Underground

The chill of the morning air hit Malcolm's lungs like a freight train. The cold filling his chest could not distract him from the earth-shattering shock of seeing her face again. Glancing back into the building with a tense jaw, he watched as Victoria and Elizabeth spoke to each other awkwardly. He couldn't remove his gaze from Elizabeth's long golden hair.

In spite of his vicious words, clenched fists, and violent outbursts, there was absolutely no anger in his heart.

He wanted to feel fury at what she had done. He needed his rage to shield him and keep him safe. But as much as he tried, it simply wouldn't come. All he felt was longing as the memories of his love for his lost wife resurfaced with a vengeance. Finally, he turned away, unable to bear the weight of his emotion any longer. He turned his focus toward the news Elizabeth had brought to him: Claire was missing and in danger.

Olivia Noble

The very thought made his already racing heart beat so hard he thought it might burst. He seized that fury, allowing it to flow through him like a river. It was all he could do not to lose his sanity. He sighed and shook his head, clearing it of any remaining foolish emotion. There was no time to think about the pain Elizabeth had caused him.

A gentle hand touched Malcolm's shoulder and he quickly turned around, eager to see Elizabeth's baby blue eyes. A mixture of disappointment and relief passed through him as he met with Victoria's soft brown irises instead. Shame welled up in his chest at these feelings and he averted his gaze.

"I'm sorry, champ," she gently said. "I can't imagine what you must be going through."

Malcolm took her hand in his. "I'll be fine," he said stoically. "This was a huge blow to me, but I don't have time to be angry with her. You were right. If her story is true, then she's just as much a victim in this situation as I am. I need to focus on the real enemy: Brantford."

Victoria smiled slightly, placing her free hand on Malcolm's cheek. "Let's go inside, get warm, and figure out a plan. There is no way that I'm letting either one of you lose any more than you already have."

Her words stunned Malcolm, causing him to stare at her in amazement. He hadn't expected Victoria to be handling this situation as well as she was. "Thank you," he said softly. "You truly are a treasure."

"This is what I do," she said with a hint of sadness. "I bring families together. I just want it to end well this time."

"It will," he said with determination, reaching out to brush a wayward strand of her hair. He wanted to kiss her, but felt uncomfortable with Elizabeth watching. "We'll make sure it does."

Victoria struggled to keep up as she followed Malcolm back inside. He moved with quick, fierce steps as he headed toward Elizabeth. When Malcolm stood before his wife, the intensity of the look he gave the poor woman was frightening.

Victoria felt her heart ache as she gazed between Elizabeth and Malcom. It was impossible to deny the pain and love she saw pass through them. She felt as if she was watching two penguins separated by a massive storm suddenly finding one another again. The sight was both beautiful and tragic all at once; she had to avert her eyes to keep from crying.

What am I thinking? Victoria asked herself in

shock. This was the woman that had ripped Malcolm's heart out. The one that made him so bitter and angry that the only way he could allow himself to be with another woman was through impersonal anal sex. A fact that she had been painfully reminded of the night before. The discomfort in her ass made her scowl and feel a little sick. Elizabeth was responsible for Malcolm's odd fetish and her damaged rear end.

"We're going to need a plan," Malcolm said. "I'll have to speak with your *other* brother, to see if there are any new developments. Perhaps we can ask the FBI for help. The child abduction might be taken more seriously this time around."

Victoria pulled her mind away from her thoughts and focused on Malcolm's words. How could she be getting jealous or feeling like an outsider when there was something much more important going on? The life of a little girl.

His little girl.

"Cameron is working with you?" Elizabeth asked brokenly. "God, I haven't seen him since my *accident*." She nearly choked on the word, with helplessness painted all over her face. "I'm so sorry for this, Mal. I was just trying to keep everyone safe. Now look at us."

"I know," he said in a hushed tone. "I won't ever forget the pain you've caused me."

"I can't expect you to," Elizabeth said, turning her gaze away. "I just want to find our baby."

Malcolm nodded. "Well, now you know how I've felt for five years."

Elizabeth looked back into his face, a tempest of anger and fear storming in her eyes. "Yes," she said with agony. "I suppose I do."

Although Victoria's reporter instinct told her that the woman before her was telling the truth, her panic and jealousy were beginning to twist her perception. As much as she fought against the emotions, she could not bear the thought of losing Malcolm again. Victoria wanted to scream in protest and tell Malcolm not to trust Elizabeth, but she knew that this would be immature and unhelpful. "We need to get back on task," she finally said, unable to remain quiet any longer. "Going to Cameron is a good idea, but perhaps we shouldn't officially go to the FBI. Brantford might have other contacts there and we don't want to tip him off. You know I'll use every asset at my disposal to find her. Between the four of us? We can find your little girl."

Malcolm squeezed Victoria's waist gently, pulling her into him. "You're right," he said softly. "We can discuss the past at another time, Elizabeth." His face became hard as he gazed into his estranged wife's eyes. "In fact, perhaps we shouldn't at all."

Elizabeth hesitated before nodding. "Maybe you're right. I'm sorry that I reopened old wounds and that I'm causing you pain. I just don't have anywhere else to go."

Malcolm lifted his hand, waving it dismissively. "Don't be sorry," he said with a sigh. "You're not the enemy here. I realize that maybe you never were. All that matters now is getting Claire back. Coming to me was the right decision."

Elizabeth offered a thin lipped smile. "A decision I should have made a long time ago," she said, lifting her chin in determination. "But there isn't anything we can do about that now. I won't let my past foolishness ruin our lives more than it already has."

Victoria felt her stomach twist up into a knot as she looked into Elizabeth's eyes. The woman was in complete anguish, even as she stood up proudly. She found herself admiring Elizabeth for the strength she saw in those crystal blue eyes. *I don't think I could ever deal with this the way these two can. Their rich man's world is so full of danger, tragedy, and heartache. I don't think I belong here.*

Chapter Two

Elizabeth sat nervously in Malcolm's high rise office as Victoria worked furiously on her laptop. She could not help feeling a little intimidated by the young reporter, and she tried to look around and study the building instead of Victoria's perfect young body and intelligent face. It was no wonder that Malcolm had fallen for her. Trying to fight back tears, Elizabeth stared at the large glass windows and tried to admire the architecture.

She had known that her husband had done well for himself in the years she had been gone, but she was still impressed with how far he had come. A small smile crossed her lips as she recalled his first office: a small dilapidated shack in a run-down part of the city. It had been all he could afford, and he had stubbornly refused her financial help. Memories of surprising him for lunches and ending up bent over his desk filled her mind, causing a pleasurable shiver to run down her spine. *How I wish those times never ended, my love,* she thought to herself sadly.

"Elizabeth?" said a familiar voice.

The sound pulled her from her thoughts and she turned to see Cameron walking into the room with Malcolm. "Baby brother," she gasped, tears pricking the back of her eyes as she quickly rose to her feet. She briskly walked over to him and threw her arms around him tightly, burying her head into his chest. "I've missed you so much."

"We have a lot to catch up on," he replied softly, holding her close. "Malcolm told me what happened. We'll find Claire, I promise."

"We're going to need that determination," Malcolm said in a low voice. "What were you able to find out?"

Elizabeth turned to look at Malcolm, and for a moment she was unable to stop herself from getting lost in his eyes. Then she was painfully reminded that he was no longer hers as he gently placed his hand on Victoria's shoulder, causing the young reporter to lift her eyes from her laptop.

Cameron frowned deeply. "I wasn't able to locate my brother at all," he said in exasperation. "However, I tapped your phone and my sister's and set them up to run a trace in case Brantford calls."

Malcolm nodded slowly as he placed his palm against his forehead. "That'll have to do for the moment. We need to get ahead of this and fast. Time is not a luxury that we have."

"If he does call and demand your surrender, champ, how do you plan to deal with it?" Victoria asked with a furrowed brow.

"I don't know," he responded softly. "I doubt he will fall for me being the bait again."

Elizabeth shuddered as she listened to the conversation. She hated that this was happening to him and that he even needed to consider risking his own life, again. "Maybe I can reason with him," she said softly, knowing that it was impossible even before she spoke.

Cameron placed a gentle hand on her shoulder, squeezing it softly. "I wish Brantford was a man that could be reasoned with, sis, but we both know he isn't."

"I know," she said sadly, turning away from her brother. "I just can't believe he would do something like this. I know firsthand how much of a bastard he really is, but he's always been so kind to Claire. Even though he hates my husb—" she stopped herself, looking at Malcolm with a frown. "Even though he hates Malcolm, the thought of him really hurting Claire is unthinkable."

"He was kind to me for a while in the beginning as well, remember?" Malcolm pointed out. "Until I realized he was really trying to sow the seeds of doubt in my mind about us. That's when his true colors showed and now we're here."

Elizabeth nodded solemnly. "He's still my brother, Mal. I don't want to lose either of you."

Malcolm stood up from his seat and slowly walked over to her. "I'm afraid he's made that impossible," he said slowly. "You know that."

She stepped closer to him, wondering if she could dare be bold enough to hug him. Just one hug couldn't hurt? She needed it more than she had ever needed anything. Elizabeth reached out tentatively, letting her arms lightly encircle his neck. She stared into his eyes with permission, deathly afraid that he would push her away.

When Malcolm awkwardly placed his hands on her back to accept the hug, she felt a sob shake her chest. She let her head fall against his shoulder, and took comfort in the arms of the man she loved. The father of her child. His familiar scent filled her nostrils, stirring her ancient longing. It had been so many years; the power of the pent-up emotion caused her whole body to shake. "This is madness, Mal," she said, as tears began to cascade down her cheeks. "Pure fucking insanity."

Malcolm took a deep breath as he held her tighter. It was unsettling how natural and comfortable it felt to have her in his arms. He felt the urge to cradle her close, and stroke her hair soothingly. He wanted to kiss her tears away and steal all her pain with his touch, but he remembered that Victoria was in the room. He remembered that things were no longer the way they used to be. He swallowed back a lump of pain as he began to gently massage between Elizabeth's shoulder blades to ease her stress. "I wish it was simpler, Lizzy. I wish none of this had ever happened."

"It's not your fault," she said softly as she reluctantly pulled herself away from him. "It's mine for being too weak to stand up to him."

"I wouldn't go that far," Victoria chimed in. "I know my opinion doesn't count for much, but your brother is fucking terrifying." She sighed as she closed her laptop. "Let's not play the blame-game and just agree that Brantford is a first class monster and figure out a way to win."

Elizabeth smiled softly. She was impressed with the younger woman, and glanced up at Malcolm. It pained her to see that he had moved on but she couldn't blame him. It gave her solace to see that he had chosen someone strong. "You're right," she agreed. "But that's the difficult part. I've never known my brother to lose at anything. Mal is the only one to have ever gotten under his skin."

"He has a way with people," Victoria joked.

Elizabeth chuckled despite the seriousness of the situation. "I see you've also noticed that about him."

"I am right here, you know," Malcolm said in mock irritation.

The room was quickly filled with the sounds

of laughter. Elizabeth looked at the man she had married, and gently lifted her hand to press her palm against his cheek.

"If I were a betting woman," she said gently, "I'd pick you over my brother any day."

"Good," he said as his lips pulled into a half smile. "Because you would be disappointed otherwise. Brantford isn't going to get away with what he has done."

His words filled her with hope. It hurt to be an enemy of her brother but she knew that his obsession had gone too far. She used to think that she would somehow be able to save him but recent events proved how foolish she really was. "He has a few safe houses that he moved Claire and me around in constantly. You were at the one in Argentina but there are others in Paris, Rome and Moscow."

"It a place to start," Cameron said. "I'll get some agents I can trust to go investigate each one. Knowing Brantford, he has several more you don't know about, but perhaps he slipped up and left a clue."

"Start with the one in Rome," Elizabeth suggested. "It's where we last were."

A sudden ringing pierced the air, causing all of them to jump in surprise. Malcolm lifted his hand to hush them all as he picked up the receiver.

"Cage," he said sharply.

Elizabeth stared at her husband's face as it

twisted into anger and hate. Malcolm pressed the speaker button on the little black box and set the receiver down in its resting place.

"Well, this is a nice little reunion isn't it?" Brantford's snide voice said gleefully. "I thought I felt my ears burning. Were you talking nasty about me, dear sister?"

"Nothing more than you deserve," Elizabeth said, her knuckles white with fury as she gripped the table. "I want my little girl back."

"That's too bad," Brantford said through a chilling chuckle. "Because I have her and I'm not giving her back until I get what I want."

Cameron remained silent as he pulled out his phone. He nodded to Malcolm, signaling that his trace was in progress. Malcolm silently thanked the man and cleared his throat.

"There are only two ways this is going to end, Brantford," Malcolm said, struggling to keep his voice even. "You can release Claire and *maybe* we can find a way to end this madness before anyone else has to die. Or, you can keep being insane and I put you down like the rabid animal you've become."

Brantford chortled in response. "Silly dog. We both know your bark is much worse than your bite. Surrender to me and I give you my word everyone in that room, including your reporter cunt, can live. Aren't I such a nice guy?"

Elizabeth felt herself flinch as she heard the

two men speak. She glanced around to the others in the room. Victoria was taking notes furiously, Cameron was monitoring the call, and Malcolm sat stoically as he spoke to her insane brother.

I'm fucking worthless, she thought bitterly. "No, Brant," she said through gritted teeth. "Enough is enough!" She was nearly at the point of screaming as her voice tore at her throat. "If you ever loved me or my daughter, you will leave her out of this. Are you really a monster or are you my big brother?" She didn't know why she was even trying to reason with him but she felt that she had to try.

"You want to talk to me about love, dear sister?" Brantford said, suddenly cold. "You ran away from our home to live with a mongrel and you even bore his spawn. You abandoned us! Now you're there with him again instead of where you belong."

Before she could speak again, a soft hand on her shoulder distracted her. She looked up to see Malcolm looming over her, his face contorted in rage.

"You leave me no choice, Brantford," Malcolm said coolly. "I will not surrender myself and I *will* save my daughter. Then I'm going to settle our score once and for all."

"I would love to see you try, dog. We'll see how well that plays out for you a second time," Brantford said with a sinister cackle. "Just to make things more interesting, I'm giving you a deadline. You have forty-eight hours to find her or surrender your worthless life—choose wisely!"

"I want to hear her voice," Malcolm said as calmly as he could.

"Fine, fine," Brantford said in annoyance. "She's right here. Say hi to mommy and daddy!"

A soft sniffling could be heard over the phone but no one spoke.

"Aren't you going to say hello? What a rude girl," Brantford said in disgust. "Not surprising considering your father is... *ow!*" he exclaimed. "You little bitch." A hard smacking sound echoed over the phone, and a low growl escaped his throat.

"Claire!" Malcolm and Elizabeth shouted in unison.

"Gag her!" Brantford ordered an unseen figure. "For that little stunt of hers, I'm making it twenty-four hours before I put a bullet in her pretty little skull. Right through the eye!"

A bone-chilling hysterical laugh escaped the madman's throat, and continued until Malcolm ripped the box from the wall, and smashed it against the floor. He bent over, picking up a small listening device from the remains of the phone and crushed it in his hand.

"Did you get a location?" he asked, his eyes storming as his body trembled.

Cameron nodded. "Just barely," he said in a

shaky voice. "Jesus… I never knew how far gone he really was."

"Your little girl is as tough as her parents," Victoria said encouragingly. "When we save her, we'll have to make sure she gets a really big allowance."

Elizabeth wanted to snap in anger at the young woman but bit her tongue. She knew that Victoria was only trying to lighten the mood, and the effort was appreciated. "Where is he?"

Cameron hesitated. "If this is correct, and I'm not sure I can trust the trace, he's here in Chicago. It looks like his office building uptown."

Malcolm began to pace around quickly. "We can't afford to be wrong," he said softly to himself. "I want people looking into every single known safe house of Brantford's and more people figuring out where he might be."

"That's a lot of ground to cover in a day," Cameron said softly. "That could be anywhere in the world."

"Then *look* everywhere in the world," Malcolm demanded. "Do whatever it takes. I'm going to find a way to get into that building and get my daughter out."

"I'm coming with you," Elizabeth said quickly.

Malcolm hesitated as his gaze fell onto her. She locked eyes with his, channeling all of her wrath through her stare.

"I would argue with you but we don't time to waste," he said softly.

The tension broke between them and she felt her lips pulling into a thin, tight smile. "What's your plan?"

"I'm going to speak with some friends," he said cryptically. "You might want to head to my home for the time being."

"No," she said stubbornly. "I'm going with you. Otherwise you'll leave me behind and charge in there on your own."

"I'm glad it's not just me he tries that crap with," Victoria said lightly.

"I like her," Elizabeth said through a tiny smirk. "Poor Malcolm. It warms my heart that you still can't fool anyone."

Malcolm rolled his eyes, releasing a sigh. "Whatever," he muttered. "Stubborn women."

Victoria and Elizabeth shared a smile as Malcolm walked away toward the elevator. "Thank you," Elizabeth said softly.

"No problem," Victoria replied with a wink. "Us girls have to stick together."

Olivia Noble

Chapter Three

"Do you really think you can use that chip to track down Brantford?" Cameron asked Victoria skeptically as they headed toward the elevators.

Victoria glared at him. "If I say I can do it, I can. I have the equipment at my apartment."

"Okay," Cameron said with a shrug.

"Just trust her," Elizabeth said to her brother. "We need to do everything we can to find my daughter."

"Our daughter," Malcolm corrected. As Elizabeth and Cameron stepped into the elevator, Malcolm stopped Victoria with a gentle touch to her arm. She turned around and looked at him with questioning eyes.

"I need Victoria to stay behind for a moment," he said quietly.

Victoria's eyebrows knitted together as she nodded.

"We'll wait downstairs," Cameron said as the elevator doors closed. He turned to chat with his sister as they started their descent to the lobby. Malcolm placed his hand behind Victoria's back, pulling her toward him.

"I'm sorry, my treasure," Malcolm said sincerely. "About Elizabeth... I never thought something like this would happen."

She shook her head. "It's not your fault. You couldn't have known."

He frowned slightly and leaned down to kiss her forehead. "I can only imagine how stressful this must be for you." His own feelings were a conflicted mess. He knew he hadn't been there for Victoria since his estranged wife had shown up.

"I admit," she said carefully, "that I am worried. Her story really sounded true and I don't think she is a world class actor." Her voice tried to remain even and objective, not letting any of her emotions slip through. "She's beautiful, Malcom. And really nice. I would understand if you wanted to..."

Malcolm cut her off with a deep kiss. His lips crashed against hers, communicating his wishes clearly. His arms wrapped around her waist and he lifted her up off the ground. Victoria was caught off guard by his passions, but quickly melted into his touch. The sweet sounds of mutual bliss filled the office.

"Victoria," Malcolm whispered. "You have

nothing to worry about. Elizabeth is in my past, but you are my future. Once this is all over, we can make our new beginning."

She looked up at him with a quivering lip, tears of relief forming in the corner of her eyes. It wasn't until he spoke these words that she realized how much fear she had been holding back. In just a kiss, he sealed away all her dark thoughts. "Malcolm," she said softly. "I would never ask you to pick me over her. I would understand."

"I know." He leaned forward, pressing his lips to hers again. "You would never have to ask. The answer is clear in my mind: you." His hand wandered up her back, easily unhooking her bra.

She gasped as she felt his hands on the bare skin of her breasts. Her nipples hardened instantly and a moan escaped her lips. "Malcolm," she whispered breathlessly. "What about Claire?"

"I need a few minutes with you to refresh my mind, or I won't be able to focus," he explained.

"Men have excuses for everything, don't they?" she asked.

He chuckled against her skin, his teeth sinking into the soft flesh of her neck. "Yes."

"Mal," she groaned. "You're really sure about this? Right now?" Her eyes softened as she gazed upon his, noticing the tense furrows in his brows and the subtle tremors in his shoulders.

"Yes," he whispered softly. "I need you." He placed his lips against her skin, kissing down her body in an agonizingly slow trail. He skillfully undid her pants, slipping them off the curve of her ass until they were down around her ankles.

The air was cold on her naked body and her nipples were painfully hard. Malcolm's lips made her skin tingle in warmth for a moment before the chill set back in. It left her feeling vulnerable and aroused all at the same time.

He got on his knees before her, pushing her back until she was sitting on his desk. Gently, he spread her legs and kissed her inner thighs.

"What are you doing?" she asked with a raised brow.

"Making this last," he said gently. His lips were achingly close to her glistening pussy. He breathed in deeply, inhaling her intoxicating scent.

A subtle smile crossed her lips. "It's okay," she said soothingly. "We're going to have all the time in the world once we find Claire."

His stormy eyes were both hard and vulnerable at the same time as he looked up at her. She knew he really did need this and a part of her did as well. *Just a few moments,* she said to herself as she brushed her hands through his hair.

"I wouldn't be able to get through this without you," he said in between gentle kisses on her thigh.

Victoria threw her head back in ecstasy as Malcolm's tongue slid across her wet slit. She could feel the rough texture of his tongue gently massaging her outer labia, and sliding across her clit. A moan escaped her lips and she opened her legs wider, allowing him more access. Her entire body was set on fire, and only more of his touch could soothe her. Eagerly she rocked her hips back and forth, trying to get even more of his tongue against her.

His fingers splayed her lips wide, allowing her wetness to flow out of her freely. He drank in the taste of her, probing his tongue into her. He lapped at her juices and swirled his tongue between her folds, exploring every inch of her with expert precision. Each and every masterful stroke of Malcolm's tongue brought Victoria closer and closer to her building orgasm.

"God, that feels amazing," she gasped. "What's gotten into you?"

He hummed a chuckle against her clit, sending pleasurable vibrations through her body. His hands grasped her from behind, pulling her tightly against his face. He started attacking her clit with his tongue, flicking it across her sensitive spot with long, quick strokes. Her legs tightened around his head in pleasure as she began to moan uncontrollably.

"Malcolm!" she cried out as her pleasure built. "It feels so good. Don't stop."

He kept up his pace, slipping a finger in between her folds. Her muscles clenched around the invading digit and she sighed in pleasure. His tongue against her clit and a finger probing her depths was making her entire body tremble in pleasure. He added a second finger, stretching out her tight muscles to prepare her for what was to come. In long, slow thrusts he pleasured her sensitive g-spot, drawing moans from her throat. His free hand slid up her back and around her body until his hand grasped at the soft flesh of her breast. His fingers expertly kneaded at her soft globes, making her groan and squirm against him.

She looked down into his face, meeting his eyes. She ran her fingers through his thick hair and she pulled his face deeper into her pussy. "You're doing and excellent... job... of... fuck that feels good." Forcing her legs apart, she lifted her ass off of his desk and ground her hips against Malcolm's face. Eagerly he matched her tempo, pumping his fingers in and out in deep thrusts. His tongue increased the pressure against her clit causing her orgasm to reach a breaking out.

"Yes, yes, yes, Malcolm!" She screamed out as every inch of her body clenched up in intense pleasure. Her back arched without her permission and her legs clenched around Malcolm's head so tightly that she was afraid of hurting him.

A long moment passed before her pleasure ebbed away. She was left a hot puddle of bliss on his desk, her chest rising and falling rapidly. He stood up, wiped his mouth with a handkerchief and began stripping his clothing. Her eyelids fluttered open to see her god of a man standing there with a proud erection. Her tongue darted out to lick her lips, wetting them in anticipation.

"What are you waiting for?" she asked softly, spreading her legs wide to encourage him.

"Just admiring you, my treasure," he replied gently. "I love everything about you, with all of my heart."

Her dark cheeks were stained with a slight blush. "Malcolm. I'm the lucky one."

"Even while getting shot at and almost dying in the jungle?" he asked with a sly smile. His fingers slid up her leg, gently massaging her healing wound.

She could feel the warmth and love in his touch. If there was any doubt left in her mind that things would end between them, he was making it rapidly evaporate. "Yes," she said seriously. "I don't care how messed up my life has become since meeting you. As long as you're with me, I know we can do anything."

He leaned down and kissed her deeply as he slid in his throbbing cock inside of her. He laid her down against his desk as he began to thrust his hips against her body. Her legs wrapped around his waist and she pulled him into her, trying to get closer than humanly possible.

"Do you really want *me?*" she asked brokenly.

Malcolm halted his thrusts for a moment to

look deeply into her eyes. She knew his answer even before her spoke.

"Yes, my treasure," he said in low voice. "Only you."

Victoria felt tears prick the back of her eyes and she clutched Malcolm against her tightly. She still didn't know what to say, and she tried to hide her emotion against his chest.

Malcolm kissed the top of her head and held her close, their bodies still connected. When she opened her eyes to look up at him, she saw the traces of moisture on his face as well. She knew that seeing Elizabeth had shaken him up, and he probably needed this release more than he was letting on.

"Don't stop now, champ," Victoria said softly, running her hands over his chest and grinding her hips against him.

Malcolm grunted in response, beginning to thrust again and picking up his pace. She could feel him swelling up inside of her and she focused on clenching the muscles of her walls around his cock. He groaned in response, pumping his hips faster and harder.

"I want to taste you again," Victoria moaned.

Malcolm's body trembled as he thrust into her over and over again. "I'm close," he groaned as he pulled out of her.

Victoria slid to her knees quickly as Malcolm's seed exploded from the tip of his cock.

Olivia Noble

She took it into her mouth, wrapping her lips around his shaft as he continued to pump his release into the back of her throat. A moan escaped from her as his hardness pulsed between her lips. She slowly pulled away.

"I do love the way you taste," she said in a husky tone, "Thanks for not making a huge mess of me."

Malcolm looked down at her with a sly smile on his face. "If there was more time, I would have."

"Just don't die, and we'll have the time in the world, champ," she said fondly as she rose to her feet.

Malcolm wrapped his arms around her, pressing his naked body against hers. "I won't, my treasure. We'll get through this."

"Please don't go charging into Brantford's office," she softly pleaded with him. "Let me do my job and figure out where he is first."

"I will give you a few hours, but then I need to try," Malcolm said in determination. "I won't let him hurt my daughter."

She nodded in understanding. Her arms wrapped around him tighter and she pressed her body against his. Taking in a deep breath, she allowed his manly scent to fill her nostrils and felt her body melt into his. Gentle kisses were placed on his shoulder as she hugged him against her. Finally she said, "I'm afraid that this will be the beginning of the end."

Malcolm gently stroked her back with his large, strong hands. "The only thing that's going to end, Victoria, is this fucking nightmare."

Chapter Four

Victoria dug her heel into the floor of her car as she pressed her foot into the pedal. The metal vehicle sped through the streets, dodging other cars in smooth motion. She enjoyed the sense of feeling unstoppable and being at peace.

"You really don't know the meaning of speed limit, do you?" Cameron asked, sounding slightly afraid.

She only laughed in response as she rounded a corner, heading back to her apartment. "There isn't exactly time to pace ourselves," she rationalized.

"Yes, but ending up dead in a burning car doesn't help anyone either," Cameron countered.

Victoria rolled her eyes. "Keep your panties on. We'll arrive at my apartment soon." She let some of the pressure off the gas as she smoothly turned another corner.

The hum of the wheels excited her and took

her mind off of the fact that Malcolm was currently with Elizabeth. She knew it was foolish to be bothered by it but she just couldn't help it. Malcolm clearly still loved his wife and she loved him just as much.

"Are you alright?" Cameron asked in concern.

"I'm fine," she said quickly.

"You missed your turn," Cameron pointed out. "Are you sure you're alright?"

A flush of heat stained her cheeks. She had been lost in her thoughts and not paying enough attention. "I suppose I have a lot on my mind," she admitted softly, "but I'm alright."

"Is it because my sister walked back into Malcolm's life?" he asked gently.

She sighed. "That and I feel like crap for even worrying about it when there is a little girl's life at stake. What's wrong with me?"

"Nothing," Cameron said, putting his hand over hers comfortingly. "I think it's only natural that we worry about losing the things and people important to us."

The warmth of his hand over hers was welcome and calming. As she turned the car around, she glanced over at him with a small smile. "That makes me feel a bit better," she said softly. "But if it's all the same, I'd rather not talk about it. I want to be focused on finding Claire."

He nodded in understanding. "I just want to

make sure that you're alright. That's all."

Her lips pulled into a broader smile and she squeezed his hand in appreciation. "Thank you, but I promise you that I'm alright. The way I figure it, Malcolm is either going to go back to his wife, or he's going to stay with me. Either way, I think I would be happy."

"Oh? That's an interesting response," Cameron said dubiously. "Are things not that serious between you and Malcolm?"

She laughed. "They are. At least, I think they are. He asked me to move in with him last night," she said through a smile, remembering how he had pretended to propose to her. "But I want him to be happy. I would be okay with him rekindling his relationship with your sister as long as it was right for him."

"That is a remarkably mature thing to say," Cameron said in approval. "If more people thought that way, we wouldn't be in this situation."

She turned her head to look at him, her brow arched curiously. "Why do you say that?"

"Think about it," he began to reason. "If Malcolm or my brother were willing to give up what they wanted for the sake of someone else, they wouldn't be fighting a duel to the death. Now that doesn't mean that I think Malcolm is wrong to fight. I absolutely think he should, but my point still stands."

Her lips formed a deep, almost painful frown.

"Do you think I'm weak?"

Cameron vigorously shook his head. "Of course not," he said quickly. "I think it takes a great deal of strength to know when to let go instead of fight."

"Well, I have no intention on simply letting go," Victoria said with determination. "I love Malcolm and I'm not going to give him up. However, if he chooses a different path, I would still support him. As a friend."

Cameron nodded. "Very admirable. Anyway, tell me again why we are going to your apartment?"

"I need some equipment to try and locate Brantford," Victoria explained. "I also want to let my roommate Chloe know that I may be gone for a while. I don't want her to be worried sick like last time."

"I think that's wise," Cameron said in agreement. "But what will you tell her?"

Victoria sighed. She hated keeping secrets from her best friend, but this was unavoidable. "Only the basics. Suddenly, I understand the whole *need to know* crap the government spews out when they are asked difficult questions."

"It alienates us from the people we want to protect, but we do it anyway," Cameron said sadly. "I'm sorry you're in a position where you need to keep secrets."

She shrugged. "Maybe when all of this is

over, I'll tell her. Lord knows it would make the greatest article ever told. The secret life of billionaires!" She didn't mean to sound as sarcastic and bitter as her voice betrayed, but it was difficult for her sense of journalistic integrity.

"I don't think anyone would believe you," he replied softly. "Hear no evil, see no evil."

Victoria shrugged as she pulled the car to a stop in front of her apartment. "It doesn't matter if they believe me or not. You don't go into investigative journalism to hunt for fairy tales that are easy to swallow. You go in for the hard truth and you never print something you can't prove."

"Easy there, Miss Chase, I meant no offense." Cameron said through a smile, raising his hands in surrender.

Her eyes rolled as she stepped out of the car but she couldn't keep her lips from forming a tight smile when he wasn't looking. "You can wait here or come up. It's up to you, I shouldn't take very long."

"Might as well come up," he offered. "Mal would kill me if something happened to you because I was too afraid to go out into the cold for a bit."

Victoria laughed good-naturedly. "I think I can handle going up into my apartment to get my laptop."

Cameron stepped out of the car, pulling his jacket tightly around him. "Let's just hurry this up.

I hate the cold."

She felt her smile broaden as she walked toward her apartment. Having Cameron around provided a sense of comfort that she hadn't expected. She even imagined that she could consider him a friend. The thought was somewhat amusing, as she recalled their odd meeting. *Every time I think my life can't get any more screwed up, it does. Being friends with a guy that shot someone at point blank range and covered me in brain matter? Just another day,* she thought to herself as she walked into the building.

Stepping inside of her apartment felt like walking into a spa. The scent of various burning candles filled the air with cloying potency.

"Chloe," Victoria said as she stepped through the threshold. "What's going on?"

Cameron followed behind her, closing the door as he entered the domicile. No one responded to Victoria's voice, so the pair of them walked into the living area. There, they found Chloe and Dominic entangled in a passionate embrace on the sofa with very little clothing.

"Ooh la la," Cameron said as he looked at the passionate couple.

"What the hell!" Chloe shrieked in surprise, pulling a pillow from the couch to cover her exposed breasts.

"This is not the worst position I've ever found you in," Victoria remarked lightly. "Hello

Dominic."

"Victoria," he greeted casually. "If I didn't know any better, I'd say you were just trying to see me naked."

Her lips tightened into a small smile. "Maybe in another life," she said in jest. "I think you have your hands full enough in this one."

"Why are you even home? I thought you were going to be with Malcolm or at work," Chloe said, her face blushing the shade of her crimson hair. She turned to look at Cameron and her face became even more mortified. "Oh god, and now I'm meeting someone for the first time like this."

"Don't worry about it," Cameron assured her kindly. "This is much better than how Victoria and I met. I'm Cameron by the way."

"Chloe," she responded as she stood up, quickly walking toward her bedroom. "What's going on, Vica?"

"I just came to grab a few things, and let you know I might be gone until the end of the week," Victoria said through a smile. "You'll have the apartment all to yourself."

Dominic looked over at Cameron with a raised brow. "Don't I know you?"

"Probably. I'm Elizabeth's brother and currently working with Malcolm," Cameron said flatly.

"And just what are you working with him on?" Dominic asked in a low voice, clearly agitated.

Cameron remained calm as he said, "Finding my niece. My brother has gone completely insane and she's in danger."

Dominic stiffened. "Fuck," he hissed. "Dammit. I need to go. Now. Tell Chloe I'm sorry," he said hurriedly.

Chloe stepped out of her room in time to hear the end of his sentence. "Sorry that you're bailing on me? Again?" Chloe asked, standing in the doorway with fury in her eyes. "And I bet you aren't going to tell me why either."

"Babe—" Dominic stammered out.

"Don't you dare," Chloe said furiously. "Just get out."

"But…"

"Out!" she demanded, pointing toward the door. "We're done, Dominic. I'm sick of this."

Dominic's face twisted up into pain and he looked as if he wanted to say something. He turned on his heel and quickly put on his clothes before briskly walking out of the apartment.

"Damn him," Chloe said, tears forming in the corners of her eyes. "He always does that."

"Maybe," Victoria said hesitantly. "Don't quite be so hard on him. I don't think he means to hurt you."

"I get that things come up at work," Chloe said, taking a deep breath to fight back her emotions. "But he isn't open with me about what is going on. He acts like I'm a child that needs protecting and I'm just done with it."

Victoria felt horrible about the circumstances and the urge to stay and comfort her friend was overwhelming. However, she knew that she couldn't and that only made it worse. Her eyes looked into Cameron's and they shared an expression of guilt.

"You're right," Victoria said softly. "He's being a jerk. Why don't we grab some afternoon ice cream and watch some sappy TV?"

Chloe's lips turned into a small smile. "No," she said with a sigh. "I appreciate the offer but I know you have things to do. I don't know what it is but I know it's important."

"Doesn't that make me the same as Dominic? For not telling you?" Victoria asked, feeling ashamed.

Chloe shook her head. "You're not my boyfriend, Vica. I don't tell you everything I'm doing either and that's okay. You're always here for me when I need you. Dominic hasn't been."

"I'm sorry, Chloe, is there anything I can do? I hate to leave you like this," Victoria said sadly. She walked over to her friend, and wrapped her arms gently around Chloe's neck.

"I'll be okay," Chloe said in a shaky voice. "I'm just going to go back into work. I was taking the day off and I'm sure it'll make my co-workers happy."

"Okay," Victoria said gently. "You be good. When I finish this assignment we'll have that sappy TV marathon for sure."

"Definitely," Chloe said enthusiastically. "Now shoo, you have work to do."

Chapter Five

"It's a lot bigger than I remember," Elizabeth said as she looked up at Malcolm's castle. "You certainly upgraded from our condo in the city."

"I still have that condo," Malcolm said softly. "But this is always where I wanted us to live when it was complete."

She nodded. "I didn't even know you were working on having something like this built."

A small smile formed on his lips. "It was supposed to be a surprise. Anyway, that's all in the past. Feel free to take a room for now, there is plenty of space."

"You're okay with your estranged wife sleeping under the same roof?" she asked dubiously.

He frowned slightly. The idea did make him a bit uncomfortable but he wanted to be mature about the situation. Her story had stripped him of his anger and allowed his feelings for her to resurface. It was dangerous to have her so close but with Brantford targeting her as well, there wasn't anywhere else for her to go. "Yes," he finally said.

"Thank you, Mal," she said through a smile, her eyes downcast and almost shy. "It means a lot to me that you're taking this so well."

"It's either this or start ranting and raving again," he joked. "We don't have time for the latter, so for now I feel it's best if we're adults about the situation."

She nodded quickly. "We're going to get her back, aren't we?"

He walked up close to her, and wrapped his arms around her waist, pulling her into his chest for a tight embrace. "Of course we are, Lizzy. No matter what happens, I'm going to get her back."

Malcolm enjoyed the way she clung to him silently, her head buried into his shirt. It felt good to have her in his arms, and he inhaled her familiar scent. A stirring in his loins caused his pants to tighten uncomfortably and guilt to form in his chest. *What am I doing?* he asked himself bitterly.

"Perhaps we should go inside," she finally suggested.

"You're right," he agreed. "I need to get a few things from the basement and I'll be ready to go."

"What things?" she asked, her brow rising in curiosity.

"Guns," he said calmly. "Lots of guns."

She blinked several times, as if she hadn't expected him to be so blunt about his violent intent. "I wish it wasn't coming to this."

"Wish in one hand, sit in the other, Lizzy, see which one fills up faster. You don't have to come with me."

She shook her head vigorously. "Yes I do," she said with determination. "I've spent enough time running away from this problem. I always thought I was doing what was best for you and Claire... but I wasn't."

He agreed, but it felt wrong to voice that opinion. It was clear in her eyes that she was already torturing herself over the circumstances they were now in and her part in putting them there. He didn't want to add to it with his own bitterness. Instead he just touched her shoulder in a comforting gesture. "Don't think about it right now. Just focus on making it better."

Biting her lip, Elizabeth leaned her head against the warmth of his palm. "Okay," she said simply.

The temptation to lean in and kiss his wife was powerful and he struggled to resist it. He brought forth the memories of his pain to push aside his love for her. *She wasn't there for me when I needed her,* he reminded himself. *Even though she never hated me... she still was too weak to be there.* He ripped his hand away from her face and briskly walked into his large home. There was no time to waste with his pointless lingering feelings. They could be dealt with later.

He forced his mind to focus on the task at hand as he walked through the halls toward his basement armory. He passed the firing range where he showed Victoria how to handle a firearm the night before, and the memories of their wild sex filled his head. A small formed on his lips as he allowed himself to remember the incredible encounter with the woman he loved. *Victoria has had my back no matter how difficult things became. No matter the danger to her or myself, she found a way. I can't let nostalgia ruin this,* he thought fiercely. As much as he still cared for Elizabeth, he couldn't allow himself to ever open his heart to her again.

All of Malcolm's weapons were held in a wall safe on the far back wall of the firing range. He opened his eyes wide, allowing the eye scanner to recognize his retina. An audible click filled the air as the locks of the large metal door disengaged. The door swung open on its own, revealing a gently illuminated white room that housed hundreds of different firearms.

"Christ," Elizabeth said in shock. "Are you fighting World War III?"

Malcolm chuckled softly. "It feels like it sometimes." He walked into the room and scanned over the various hand guns and rifles that lined the walls of the room. He skipped over them, walking to a locker that had several Kevlar vests inside. He stripped out of his jacket and shirt, putting the vest over his bare chest.

"Mal," Elizabeth said in approval. "I don't remember that either."

He shrugged his shoulders nonchalantly, offering her a sly half smile. "A lot has changed while you've been away, Lizzy."

"I can see that," she said with a hint of sadness. "I'm going to need one of those as well."

Malcolm agreed and handed her another vest.

"No peeking," she teased as she began taking off her clothes.

He turned his back while she changed, forcing himself to focus on the guns. It was an easy process to select which gun he wanted to take with him. The customized pair of colts that he taught Victoria with were his preferred firearms of choice. He picked up a shoulder holster and attached it to his chest before placing the guns in their respective pockets.

"You can look now," Elizabeth said softly as she wrapped her arms around him. "It's safe."

His back stiffened at first but he slowly felt himself relax into her touch. "I don't think it'll ever really be safe, Lizzy."

"Maybe not," she said sadly. "I'm glad you found someone, Mal."

"She's as special as you are," he said

sincerely. "I've invited her to live here with me."

Her arms tightened around his waist causing her soft breasts to press into his back. "I..." she began to say before the sound of Malcolm's phone cut her off. A sigh escaped her lungs as she pulled her arms away.

Malcolm offered her an apologetic look as he pulled his phone from his jacket pocket. "Cage," he said into the phone.

"Mal," said Dominic's familiar voice. "You need to get to the club as soon as you can."

Malcolm's lips formed a frown. "Is something happening there? Did the cops show up?"

"No, nothing like that. But I ran into Victoria and... what the fuck, Brantford's little brother?" Dominic said bitterly. "*They* were kind enough to inform me on what happened. So I've been running around like a madman trying to help before you go off and get yourself killed."

The hurt tone in Dominic's voice was like a knife in Malcolm's heart. "I don't know what to say, Dom," he said apologetically. "I'm sorry you found out that way. It's not as if I was intentionally keeping you in the dark."

Dominic sighed. "I know, it's just a lot of bullshit happening quickly. I pissed Chloe off by keeping her in the dark, too. This must be more karma."

"What happened?" Malcolm asked in

concern.

"Nothing that can't be talked about later," Dominic said stoically. "Just come to the club."

Malcolm turned to look at Elizabeth and a lump formed in his throat. He had opened up Club Luxe as a way to help him forget the pain that she had caused him. It felt strange to bring her to that place as a friend and he was afraid it would cause her even more pain. "I'm on my way," he finally said. There wasn't time to sugar coat his past without her. *If she wants to be a part of my life, she's going to have to deal with this eventually.*

"What was that?" Elizabeth asked curiously.

"Dominic telling me that I'm needed at my club," he said stiffly. "It sounded important, so I'm going to see what's wrong. Then we'll make a plan to get Claire back with Victoria and Cameron."

Elizabeth raised a brow. "A club?"

"It'll be easier to show you."

Chapter Six

Elizabeth wasn't sure what to expect as she walked into the underground club her husband had created. The large, frightening metal door gave her a sense of foreboding. The tunnel leading down into the main club made her feel like she was entering the belly of the beast. *Just what kind of club is this?* she wondered to herself.

As she stepped through the second set of doors into the grand hall of the club, she quickly realized just what she had walked into. People were dancing sensually to the sound of pulsing music, exploring each other with curious hands. Some were completely nude and enjoyed having sex out in the open.

"Mal?" she asked, looking at him with wide eyes.

"Club Luxe is a private swinger's club. Only the most elite can afford entry," he explained calmly. "This is just a normal night. The real events are on Fridays when I make my appearance."

"Why?" she asked, her curiosity overriding her good judgment.

He took a step closer to her, his imposing frame towering over her. Leaning down, he whispered, "Because, Lizzy. I'm the King of Kink."

His voice caused a thrill of excitement to wash over her. Droplets of her arousal formed between her thighs, dampening her panties. "I see," she gasped softly. "I don't know what to say to that. I'm glad you found a way to amuse yourself while I was gone."

He pulled away from her, a sad smile framing his strong face. "After two years, I decided that I was done being sad and killing myself with work." He looked away from her into the heart of the club. "I had all the money in the world and no one to share any of life's joys with. So I created Club Luxe, figuring that if I couldn't be happy, at least I could help others like myself find something."

His reasoning had caught her off guard. She followed his gaze to where the people were enjoying the company of one another in wild, raw passion. "I never wanted to cause you so much pain, Mal."

"Even the best of intentions can cause the worst of pain," he said sympathetically. "I understand why you left now and that does help with my anger… but not with the feeling of loss. No matter what, we lost five years of our lives."

She nodded, her hand unconsciously slipping into his. "I don't want to miss any more."

His hand squeezed hers fondly. "Then let's find Claire quickly and get on with living. I'm sick of dealing with your brother's insanity." He pulled his hand away and began walking deeper into the club.

There was an empty feeling where his hand once was. Though Malcolm was being kind and strong for her, she could see the pain she was still causing him. He refused to allow himself to be vulnerable around her like she always remembered him being. It made her wonder if he was like that with Victoria. *He must be. Mal has always worn his heart on his sleeve,* she thought to herself sadly.

She shrugged off her sadness and followed him. He navigated them through the club until she saw him approaching a familiar face by the bar.

"Speak of the she-devil," Dominic said coldly. "How nice of you to finally show up, Elizabeth."

"She's not the she-devil anymore," Malcolm said. "More of Brantford's manipulations."

"Oh," Dominic said sheepishly. "Well… this isn't awkward."

Elizabeth felt herself smile despite the

situation. "To be fair, I write a very convincing I'm-leaving-and-faking-my-own-death letter."

"You have no idea," Malcolm agreed. "Anyway, why did you call me here, Dom?"

"I'll let the others know you're here," Dominic said as he motioned for one of the bouncers to approach. "Let the guests know the king is back."

"Right away," the man said, his eyes snapping toward Malcolm. "It's good to have you back, sir."

"It's good to be back." He dismissed the bouncer with a wave and then returned his gaze to Dominic. "You know I don't like surprises, Dom."

"You'll like this one," Dominic assured him.

Malcolm looked unconvinced until the music in the room came to a stop. Everyone in the club stopped what they were doing, finally taking notice that the king was among them. Elizabeth felt the electricity humming through the air. She looked around, trying to understand what was happening.

The guests walked toward the stage, each of them stepping up onto it with hesitation. It was as if they knew it was wrong of them to do but some other driving force ushered them on. Finally, they cast their gazes down to Malcolm.

"What is the meaning of this?" he asked, his voice booming out in the silence of the club.

A middle aged man dressed in a freshly pressed grey suit approached the edge of the stage overlooking the rest of the club.

"Malcolm," he said in a resonating voice. "For these past three years you've always been good to us. Our lives are stressful and thankless but here we can relax, enjoy ourselves and be anyone we want to be. Not who we are expected to be."

Elizabeth watched the events unfold, emotion welling up in her chest at the impassioned words of the man addressing Malcolm.

"What are you getting at?" Malcolm asked in confusion as he stepped closer to the stage.

The middle aged man looked down into Malcolm's eyes, a grimace painting his face. "We've just been made aware of your situation with Brantford Cunningham. I speak for all of us when I say we want to help."

"If you know my situation than you know I can't let you do that," he said stoically. "It's against the rules."

"Damn the rules!" A handsome young man with golden eyes said.

"I agree. There is no place for rules when the daughter of our king is in danger," an identical looking man said.

"You twins are always getting into trouble," Malcolm said with dry amusement. "I'm not so foolish a man that I would cast aside aid when it comes to my daughter… but I have to think of all of you as well. It could get all of us killed."

Olivia Noble

The older man cleared his throat. "We are patrons of Club Luxe," he said resolutely. "You are the King of Kink and we are but your humble chargers." Each word was stressed out as if to make a point.

Elizabeth's eyes widened in realization. These powerful people were all choosing to lower themselves for Malcolm's sake. They were casting aside their pride and independence for his sake.

"Everyone," Malcolm choked out. "If that's how you feel, than who am I to deny you? I would be honored to accept your aid."

"We've taken the liberty of readying ourselves," one of the twins said. "Whatever you need, our king, just say the word."

Malcolm nodded firmly. "I could really use some help with these treason charges against me. A small army to get my daughter back and to make sure Brantford has nowhere to run once I find him."

"Done," the twins said in unison.

"Get to it," Malcolm ordered. "We have no time to waste. I've been given twenty-four hours to surrender myself or my daughter is killed. That was five hours ago"

"We won't let that happen," the middle aged man said. "It wouldn't be a party without our king."

"Thank you," Malcolm said sincerely as he turned away from the stage.

"You sure know how to inspire loyalty," Elizabeth said as he rejoined her at the bar. "I wasn't sure what to think of this place at first but now I couldn't be more thankful."

"It's funny how it's easy to dismiss something until you need it," Malcolm said with a twinge of bitterness.

She turned away to hide her shame. "That's not what I did to you," she said softly.

"I know. But it felt like it and I can't make that feeling go away." Malcolm placed a hand on her shoulder and gave it a comforting squeeze.

"Will it always be this way, do you think?" she asked sadly.

"I don't know but it's something we both need to deal with," he replied calmly. "I don't mean to make you sad, but it hurts that the only time I've seen you in five years is when our daughter is in danger."

She wanted to defend herself but bit her tongue. It was painful to admit to herself that her actions caused him pain, even if it had been to save his life. She knew it didn't give her the right to expect him to welcome her with open arms. "It hurts to see that you moved on without me, Mal," she said, looking up into his stormy eyes. "It hurts that I was hated by you for years and that I bring you pain just by being here."

"We can't talk about this now," he said, pulling his hand away from her. "For what it's worth, I wish I could feel differently, but I can't. I don't hate you and I don't think I ever truly did. I was just angry and that anger was a shield to protect me from the pain."

She nodded slowly. "I know, Mal. I just feel like everything is falling apart."

He sighed. "That's how I've felt for years."

He turned away, nodding to Dominic who had remained silent the entire time, pretending to be busy cleaning glasses. Tears gathered in her eyes and dripped down her face in small rivulets. An overwhelming feeling of loss caused her stomach to clench tightly, her throat to become dry, and her breathing came in short, painful waves. In an instant she saw a future with her family that could have existed but never will. She felt stupid for even considering that Malcolm would be open to picking things up where they left off.

"Lizzy," Malcolm's gentle voice sounded out. His strong arms wrapped around her, holding her close against him. "Calm down," he said soothingly.

She hadn't realized that she was hunched over, hyperventilating like a fool. "I'm sorry," she said in a scratchy voice. "I don't know what came over me. I just…"

"What can I do?" he asked softly.

She looked up into his dark eyes, filled with gentleness. Even if he wasn't hers anymore, he was still the same man she knew. "Get our baby back." She pushed herself upright and took a deep, steadying breath. "You're right, it's all that matters. I can deal with you moving on and even hating me as long as I know Claire is safe."

He nodded in agreement and took her hand into his. She focused all of her emotion on that single point of contact, as if it might create some kind of unbreakable anchor between them. For the first time in five years, she felt safe.

He led her back into a hallway that separated itself from the main part of the club. It seemed like a private section to her and it made her heart beat faster. Malcolm reached out, opening the door to some room. She peered inside as he pushed the door open, and saw the large king sized bed in the corner of the room. A small blush crept into her cheeks as her mind became filled with passionate thoughts about the man holding her hand.

"Mal?" she asked hesitantly. "What's going on?"

Chapter Seven

"I have no idea what you're doing," Cameron said as he stood behind Victoria.

She felt herself smile as her fingers danced across her laptop keyboard. The little white letters on each key were almost erased from prolonged use from her job. "I'm connecting the little chip that Malcolm found embedded into his phone to my laptop and tracing the signal that it sends back to the listening device. I'm hoping that I can narrow down Brantford's location and even track his movements."

Cameron nodded. "Well, that part I understand, but how the hell has your laptop even survived with the way you type on it?"

Victoria chuckled, keeping her focus on the screen in front of her. "Because he loves me," she said simply. "And he's going to help get free from all of this madness."

"It's a he?" Cameron asked with a raised

Billionaires Underground

eyebrow. "I thought technology was always female."

"No, that's a ship or a car. Computers are totally fair game," she explained as she made several rapid keystrokes. "Alright. I've connected the chip and turned off the ability for whoever is on the other side to be listening to us."

"Where is it?"

She looked at her screen as a globe appeared. "It's triangulating the signal," she said, leaning back into her seat. Slowly, her laptop processed the information until it zeroed in onto a map of Chicago. The address displayed was Brantford's office building. Her lips pulled into a tight smile and she subtly gripped her fist in a tiny gesture of victory.

"So he really is here," Cameron said in an uneasy tone. "Somehow that feels too easy."

"I agree." Victoria made a few more keystrokes to identify the receiving device. It was a cellphone that she hoped was Brantford's. "I'm going to remote access his phone and see if we can spy on him. Turnabout is fair play."

Cameron folded his arms across his chest. "You know, if it doesn't work out for you as a reporter, I think I could put in a word for you to be part of the FBI."

She chuckled in response. "I'll keep it in mind but I rather like being a reporter. There is something really thrilling about searching for the truth. Even if that truth isn't pretty."

"I admire that," he said through a smile.

Voices came through the speakers of Victoria's laptop as she gained access to Brantford's cellphone. The two of them froze, attempting to listen to the soft, barely audible sounds.

"This asshole isn't seriously going to let me kill his daughter?" Brantford mumbled in irritation. "Is he bluffing, or just stupid enough to think he can beat me?

Victoria's eyes widened in surprise. She expected that the remote access would work but not that they would have a rare opportunity to peer into Brantford's mind when he thought he was alone. She could swear that he sounded worried for Claire's life, a stark contrast to every interaction she'd had with him.

"I want security doubled in the building," Brantford ordered an unseen person. "Knowing that idiot, he's going to come rushing in here and start a war."

"Sir," a gruff voice said. "Are you really going to hurt the little girl?"

"Of course," Brantford said coldly. "Unless my worthless brother-in-law surrenders. It's better for her to die than see what is coming next."

"This isn't what we signed up for, sir," the voice said.

Brantford slammed something against his

desk, creating a booming noise through the speakers. "Do I pay you to have opinions?" he asked dangerously. "Double the security. Now!"

"Yes sir," the gruff voice said in a defeated, fearful tone.

The guard's footsteps echoed out of the room, leaving Brantford alone to pace back and forth. "Just surrender, you son of a bitch," he muttered to himself. "It will be easier on everyone involved." Brantford sighed, and the squeaking sound of him leaning back in his chair could be heard through the speakers.

A buzzer sounded, and a female voice spoke: "What can I do for you, Mr. Cunningham?"

"Cancel all my appointments today, Laura," he said briskly. "And come see me in my office. Make sure you're not wearing any panties."

"Yes sir," the woman said, the line going dead.

"Might as well get me some cunt before I kill—"

Victoria pressed the mute button, silencing the voices. "Okay," she said with a disgusted grimace. "I really don't need to hear the details of your brother's office brothel." A shudder ran through her body as her gaze turned to Cameron. "We need to tell Malcolm about this right away. He's going to need to know what he's up against."

Cameron nodded in agreement. "This is valuable, Victoria. We can also use this to hear how he's coordinating with his men while we go in. We could be a step ahead of him the entire time."

"I don't trust how easy this is," Victoria said, biting her lip. "But I don't want to overthink things for the sake of overthinking."

"I know how you feel." Cameron made a humming noise as the gears in his mind turned. "He could have wanted us to hear everything we just did. Which makes that information worthless at best and a deathtrap at worst."

It was a frustrating dilemma. She had been so used to dealing with a Brantford that was always seemingly two steps ahead of them. Feeling like they might actually have the advantage was strange and made her feel uneasy. "For now, our best move is to tell Malcolm and figure this out together. We don't have enough time to wonder if the information is good or not. We have to act."

"That's exactly what I'm worried about," Cameron said apprehensively. "Running out of time."

Victoria pulled out her phone and dialed Malcolm's number. She waited for several moments while the phone rang before it went to answering machine. She tried again, only to get the same results. "He's not answering," she said worriedly.

"Try Dominic," Cameron suggested.

Victoria nodded and dialed his number. In

the space of a few rings, Dominic picked up the phone.

"This is Dominic," he answered simply.

"It's Victoria," she replied. "I need to find Malcolm."

"He should be on his way to the club," Dominic said a little nervously. "Did you find anything?"

"Yes, a great deal," she said cryptically. "I'll tell you when I see you. Cameron and I are on the way."

The feeling of Club Luxe was different than Victoria remembered. It was no longer a place where rampant lust permeated the air. She sensed that the atmosphere had changed to that of people at war. Everyone wore grim faces as they talked among one another, each suggesting ways to aid Malcolm in his fight with Brantford. There was a sense of cooperation among each of the patrons as they all moved toward a singular goal.

"This is quite amazing," Cameron said in approval. "Malcolm managed to find himself some very powerful allies. I didn't expect the members of Club Luxe to rally like this."

"I didn't either," Victoria admitted. "Especially when he said that was against the rules."

Cameron grunted in response. "People like this are always trying to find a way to break the rules. Speaking as an FBI agent... some of the cases that piss me off the most are rich dick-bags that can actually get away with whatever they want."

"I thought you were a rich dick bag," Victoria teased.

"Nope. That's my brother."

"But don't you appreciate that they are on our side?"

Cameron shrugged. "They are still dick-bags. Even if they have their hearts in the right place for once."

"You really shouldn't think so poorly of them, Cameron," she said softly. "I thought that way too until I stepped into this world."

Cameron gave her a long look, his brows knitted. "And how many times have you almost died while in this world? Malcolm even blackmailed you with his resources. My brother is a maniac and normal justice won't bring him down."

Victoria frowned. "I suppose you are right. However, I would argue that just because what we are doing isn't what's considered normal or within the boundaries of the law, doesn't make it wrong."

Cameron smiled. "Speaking as the uncle of a little girl and the brother of a woman who's been through hell and back, I couldn't agree more."

Victoria shook her head, rolling her eyes in frustration. "I think you simply enjoy playing devil's advocate for the sake of it."

He shrugged his shoulders casually. "I'm told it makes me either very annoying or very charming."

"I'm leaning on the side of annoying," Victoria said, chuckling softly. "Maybe a little charming."

As they spoke, a pair of twins approached Cameron and Victoria. "My lady," they said in unison. "It's good to see you again."

Victoria wasn't sure if she should be impressed or frightened by how well the pair worked with one another. "It has been a while," Victoria said simply. "I'm glad to see the two of you are helping Malcolm."

"Of course," one said smoothly.

"He's the king," the other finished.

Cameron raised a brow. "You two wouldn't happen to be Byron and Jace would you?"

The two nodded in conformation. "We are," they both said. One twin stepped forward sadly. "We're sorry to hear about your father."

"He lived a good life," Cameron replied, his eyes glistening slightly. "And his passing was painless at the very least."

For once, Victoria was able to glean into the pain that Cameron was facing at the loss of his parent. She was so used to seeing him act stoically that it almost broke her heart to see him suffer. "Have either of you seen Malcolm?" Victoria asked, attempting to change the subject.

"Yes," one of the twins said.

"He went into his private room with a stunning blonde."

Victoria stiffened.

"I've never seen a woman with such striking blue eyes. The king surely knows how to pick unique women."

Cameron frowned. "That's my sister," he said in annoyance.

"She is a rare beauty," one of the twins complimented.

"But I prefer his choice of Victoria," the other said. "She has true spirit."

"And I prefer not to be spoken about as if I'm not here," Victoria said with a sigh. Her mind wandered to visions of what Malcolm could be doing in his private room alone with Elizabeth. *Don't be paranoid,* she chided herself. She trusted Malcolm and she was positive there was nothing to be concerned with. "Thanks for letting me know where he is. I need to speak with him."

"Don't be a stranger," the twins said as they walked away.

Victoria felt a shiver run down her spine as they disappeared from view. Even though she was with Malcolm, those two with their hypnotic golden eyes still managed to make her body respond. "Ugh," she said in frustration. "I'm never sure to be disturbed out or flattered by the two of them."

"They have always been like that," Cameron said. "I remember going to boarding school with them. They were a few grades ahead of me and would often woo the students from the all girls' school across the street. Even some of the men fell to their charms."

"Did you?" she asked teasingly, finding the thought incredibly arousing.

"Of course not," Cameron said stoically. "Come on."

A giggle escaped her throat as she led them through the halls of Club Luxe. It was so fun poking fun at Cameron; he hardly ever flinched when she pressed his buttons. She had always imagined having an older brother similar to Cameron. She was already sharing Elizabeth's husband, and she figured that it wasn't terribly inconvenient to share her brother as well. The thought was amusing and brought a grin to her lips. Eagerly, she walked towards the door of Malcolm's private sanctum within Club Luxe. She wanted to tell him what she had found and give her support in finding his daughter. Once they succeeded in their mission, the two of them could finally be together. It would be difficult at first, especially with Elizabeth coming back into his life, but they would manage.

Her fingers clutched at the handle of the door and she slowly turned the knob. A feeling of dread welled up in her chest but she forced it down. She just wanted to see Malcolm again.

But the sight that met her eyes made her blood run cold.

Malcolm stood in the center of the room with Elizabeth in his arms. His lips were pressed against hers in a passionate kiss.

"Maybe I should come back later," Victoria whispered, rage building in her stomach and spreading through the rest of her body.

The two of them separated at the sound of her voice. Elizabeth looked horrified and Malcolm had shame all over his face.

"I can explain," Malcolm said quickly. "This... fuck."

"That's right," Victoria said bitterly. "Tell me how this isn't what it looks like. I can't wait to hear how you twist your words to suit the situation."

Cameron placed his hand on her shoulder gently. She shrugged it off and turned on her heel. "You tell him what we found," she said waspishly. "I need some air."

Chapter Eight

A little earlier...

"What's going on?" Elizabeth asked as the door closed behind her.

He let out a soft sigh and cast his gaze upon her. "We need to talk," he said slowly. "This can't keep going on. It's going to get one or both of us killed if we walk into Brantford's building to save Claire, only to be distracted by our feelings."

Elizabeth looked away in shame. "I know. I don't mean to get so swept up in drama when there are bigger problems going on."

Malcolm offered her a gentle smile. "I'm not angry with you or asking you to apologize. I'd be lying to you if I said this didn't make me very emotional." He approached her and placed a hand gently on her shoulder. "So, while we have a few moments, before we go rushing into what could be a trap, let's talk."

She looked up at him with her big blue eyes and a grimace formed on her face. "I don't know what to say, Mal. I love you. I always have. I feel cheated out of the past five years."

"I feel the same way, Lizzy," Malcolm said with more bitterness than he intended. "But this was your choice."

"I..." she started to say defensively before biting her tongue. "I suppose you're right. I broke away from my brother easily enough when he took Claire, but never before."

His eyes softened. He reached out and touched her shoulder gently. "I'm sorry. I will never be able to get over that. You could have come home, Lizzy. I spent thousands of hours looking for you and millions of dollars in resources trying to get in contact. I couldn't believe that you really felt that way and I hoped against hope that something like *this* had happened." He felt his anger welling up in his chest and tried to force it down. "Maybe I could have found you sooner, but I always thought that if you knew I loved you, you would come back to me. By the time I realized you were gone for good, it was too late." His chest heaved with a mixture of emotions: anger, sadness and confusion. Tears threatened to fall from his eyes, and he lifted his sleeve to his eyes, wiping the moisture away.

She placed her hand on his face, lightly

brushing a few strands of hair behind his ear. "Mal," she said gently. "I can't imagine what you're going through. I do know that I have always kept you in my heart. I never stopped loving you, but it doesn't matter... I wasn't here. I should have been."

Malcolm placed his hand over hers. "It does feel like twisted fate, to meet now after so much has happened. However, I stand by what I told you at the house: you're important to me and I want you in my life. As a friend."

"I think I'm strong enough to deal with that. You mean a lot to me, too," she said sincerely.

"Then let's work together and stop worrying about the past. Instead, let's focus on the future and our daughter," Malcolm said with determination.

Elizabeth's lips pulled into a tight, fond smile. "Sounds wonderful," she said. Her eyes became bright and her tone was uplifted.

Malcolm remembered the brightness in her eyes. It was almost as if nothing bad had ever happened between them and they were still a happily married couple. "Lizzy," he said in a scratchy voice, filled with conflicted emotion. "Something odd just occurred to me."

"What?" she asked in a soft voice. Her feet carried her once step closer and she pressed her body into his chest, wrapping her arms tightly around his waist.

"We never did kiss goodbye that morning," he said, his lips pulling into a sad smile. "I woke up before you and left for work."

Elizabeth's cheeks turned a soft shade of pink and her heart pounded through her chest so hard that Malcolm could feel it against his.

"I was used to it," she said in a shaky voice.

"Well," he said quietly. "How would you like for us to revisit that last kiss we never had? Just for closure."

Elizabeth nodded, interlacing her fingers with his.

Taking a deep breath for strength, Malcolm leaned down and pressed his lips against hers. He had only intended for it to be a quick goodbye peck, but he felt her arms clench around him. He did not even notice when he began holding her just as tightly. Everything that he had been feeling over the past five years was flowing through his body: anger, love, elation. He poured it all into her.

She responded with her own passion, her body melting into his. Fingers dug into his back, trying to pull him even closer than he already was.

"Maybe I should come back later," the sharp sound of Victoria's voice pierced the air.

Malcolm ripped his lips from his estranged wife and cast his gaze toward the woman he loved. She had fire in her eyes so intense he could feel the heat on his skin.

"I can explain…"

"Mal," Elizabeth said in a quivering voice. "God, I'm so sorry."

With a shake of his head, Malcolm looked between Elizabeth and her brother. "This is my fault for being sentimental. I'll be right back."

He briskly walked out of the door, sliding his body past Cameron's large frame. He saw Victoria walking out of the club down the hall and hurried after her as fast as his feet would carry him.

"Wait!" he cried out as she exited through the main door into the long hallway that led to the street.

"For what?" she demanded as she turned around. Her eyes narrowed at him with pain and anger fueling her gaze.

"Victoria," he said gently. "Please, allow me to explain."

"No need," she said coldly. "I really don't want to hear how you're going to spin this story."

He set his jaw to keep from speaking, not sure of what to say in the wake of her rage. "I'm not going to do that, but you need to know that I am still yours."

"Oh really?" she asked with mocking disbelief. "Because that kiss sent a clear message to me. I meant what I told you, Malcolm. I'd have supported you if you were upfront with me. I suppose you've never shown me much respect in this relationship and it's my fault for expecting that from you."

Frustration welled up in his chest. He had never meant for this to happen. "We kissed, but…"

"Please, Mal," Victoria said softly. "Stop. I can't have this conversation right now. I'm going to help you save Claire, so don't worry. I won't let this get in the way."

Malcolm sighed and nodded in understanding. "After this is over, please talk to me. I swear to you that I love you and I meant every word this morning."

A flash of doubt crossed her eyes. "I don't think that's a good idea. I think it's better if you and I don't speak for a while. I'm sorry, Mal, but this is really hurtful."

He reached out to touch her shoulder instinctively but she recoiled from him. "Forgive me, my treasure," he said sincerely. "I can't let you just walk away from me. I care too much."

Her jaw was set in anger and her nostrils flared. She sighed, releasing the tension in her body before speaking. "I know what I saw, Mal." Her tone was distant but not as angry as her body portrayed. "Now, let's go save your daughter and you can have your family back."

A deep frown formed on his lips. "What did you find?" he asked in the most businesslike tone he could muster.

The question seemed to relax her. A professional relationship was tolerable. "That Brantford is in his office with a small army. You're going to need more people, or else you're just walking right into a trap."

"Thank you," Malcolm said softly. "The people won't be a problem. One of my friends was even able to provide a blueprint of the building."

"That we could use to sneak in," Victoria said in approval. "I'll keep listening to Brantford's movements and we can know what he's planning as he orders it."

Malcolm felt pride swell in his chest. "No matter what happens, Victoria. I will always be in your debt. You're always my friend."

A tear stained the corner of Victoria's eyes but she refused to let it fall. "Thank you," she said softly. "I hope you can pick up where you left off with Elizabeth."

"That's not going to happen," Malcolm said passionately. "I'm going to do whatever it takes in order to make this right. I love you, my treasure."

"Please don't call me that," she said in a shaky voice. "I know what I saw, Mal." She looked up into his eyes. Her dark orbs stormed with pain. "Even if you don't want to admit it to yourself. I saw two people in love."

"I never said I didn't love her," Malcolm said sincerely. "I'm not going to tell you that kiss was meaningless either. However, it didn't have the meaning you think it does."

She looked at him with skeptical eyes. "I… never mind. I said I didn't want to talk about this right now. Please, let's just get back to the task at hand."

You're an idiot, Malcolm, he mentally insulted himself. "I understand," he said, trying his best to mask his own pain. "I'm going to go get those blueprints. Be ready to go as soon as you can." He reached into his jacket and pulled out one of his colts. "I want you to have this."

She looked at it for a long moment before reaching out to gently touch the cold metal. "Is this the one you showed me how to use?"

He nodded. "I want you to keep it. Even if we never speak again after this. I want part of me to be keeping you safe."

She clasped her hand around the gun and clutched it close to her breast. "Thank you, Mal."

It was too painful to speak another word. He felt as if a part of his heart was ripped away and he was frightened he wouldn't be able to get it back. He turned on his heel and briskly walked back into the club.

Victoria meant the world to him and he was determined not to lose her. Somehow, he was going to make her understand that he was truly done with Elizabeth. The kiss he shared with her was a close on their past so that they both could have new futures

As he pushed the doors open and entered the club, all eyes turned on him. Tears threatened to rain from his eyes, and he forced them shut to keep the water at bay. He sucked in a deep breath and bellowed out, "Club Luxe!" over the sound of pulsing music.

The sounds came to a halt at once, leaving Malcolm with dead silence all around him.

"Every one of you are members of this family. Every one of you are friends that I hold dear," he said, his voice echoing in the silence. "Without you, this place would hold no meaning. However, I am sad to say that once this night is over. I will no longer be your King of Kink."

Murmurs of surprise spread throughout the room. Even he was shocked by his own words but he knew this was the right thing to do.

"What are you saying, Mal?" someone in the crowd asked.

"When my daughter is returned to me," he said with determination. "I won't have a place here any longer. I will truly miss all of you."

The twins appeared in front of him, bowing graciously. "We understand," they said in unison.

"Long live the king!" someone shouted. The others in the room joined the chant, shouting over one another to proclaim their undying loyalty.

Malcolm was taken aback by the response. He had never known how much this place meant to him until he was on the cusp of leaving it all behind. His hands rose in the air, quieting the crowd.

"I have one favor to ask before I go," he said seriously. "Never forget to party like the gods we are!"

The crowd laughed and erupted into frantic cheering. Malcolm looked around, finding Victoria standing far too close to Cameron and speaking with him in hushed whispers. Pangs of jealousy coursed through him that he quickly quashed. *I have no right.* He shook the feeling away and his gaze finally found Elizabeth's. She stood there in the middle of the crowd, looking at him with wide eyed awe. Her golden blonde hair tousled around her shoulders and a smile that managed to soothe his aching heart.

"Looks like you have them all in a frenzy," Dominic said from behind him.

Malcolm turned to look at his old friend and forced a smile. "They needed to know now. I hope you're ready to show off your scepter."

"What?" Dominic asked in surprise. "You don't mean?"

"Who else am I going to name king?" Malcolm chuckled and clapped his hand on his friend's shoulder. "But first, you should mend things with Chloe."

Dominic looked away sheepishly. "I don't know how. It's not like I can tell her about what goes on behind the scenes. At best it will scare the shit out of her and at worst it could get her killed."

Malcolm understood his friend's concerns. The Organization took its secrets very seriously. "If you love and trust her. Tell her the truth. She will understand."

"I don't want her to get hurt," Dominic said with a furrowed brow.

"You're already hurting her, Dom," Malcolm countered thoughtfully. "Think about it."

Dominic nodded slowly. "Fuck, you're right."

"I need you to do me a favor and quickly," Malcolm said in a more business like tone.

The change was noted quickly by his friend, who instantly hid away his pain. "Say the word."

"Make me an appointment to the dry cleaners after I deal with Brantford," Malcolm said through a smile. "He's never going to know what hit him."

Chapter Nine

The inside of the black van was cramped and filled with computer monitor equipment. The plan was simple; wait for law enforcement to come distract Brantford and his men while Malcolm and Victoria snuck in through an unused maintenance shaft found on the blueprints of the building.

Elizabeth rested in one corner of the van with blankets draped around her. Malcolm watched her for a moment, debating on waking her up or not. *I'll let her rest,* he decided before turning his attention onto Cameron.

"I didn't think you would be able to pull this much support from law enforcement," he commented in appreciation.

"One of your patrons at the club made it a lot easier for my bosses to take the accusations seriously," Cameron replied as he gazed into a computer screen. "I'm getting word that the search warrant is on the way."

"I really hate waiting for red tape to be cut," Malcolm said, wrinkling his nose in frustration.

Cameron turned around in his seat to face Malcolm. He looked at him with understanding eyes. "I wish we could just charge in as well but this is the best plan. Both to make sure that we bring my brother down and make sure you're alive after we save your daughter."

Malcolm sighed, releasing his pent up anxiety. "The logical businessman part of me knows that but the father in me wants to level this whole building."

"That might be counterproductive at the moment," Cameron said through a tightened jaw. "When the time comes and you have the chance to put my brother down… the boys inside know to look the other way."

Malcolm's lips formed a predatory smirk. "Good," he said coldly. "This will be over soon." His eyes studied Cameron for a moment and felt sorry for the fact that soon, he would have to kill Cameron's brother. "I am sorry it has come to this."

"Don't be," Cameron said stoically. "My brother died a long time ago. It's time to put him in the grave."

Malcolm admired how Cameron was able to keep his emotions in check despite the personal nature of the situation. "I'm going to get some air," he said after a moment. "Tell me when your people are ready to move. I'm going to wait by my position."

"Roger," Cameron said idly as he turned back around.

Malcolm opened the back of the van and stepped out onto the street. He cast his gaze towards the end of the street where a manhole covering was slightly ajar. Victoria was waiting for him down there. He wanted to be with her now but she made it clear that she wanted space from him until everything was ready.

"Mal," a soft voice said behind him.

He turned to see Elizabeth stepping out of the van behind him. Her eyes were glossed over from just waking up and she idly rubbed at them as she stood next to him. She abandoned her dress from earlier in favor of comfortable leggings and a thick winter coat over a pale blue blouse.

"Rest well?" he asked, chuckling slightly at the sight of her. The half-asleep state she was in reminded him of times past and he thought she looked just as adorable now as she did the first time he ever saw her waking up.

"Are you making fun of me?" she asked in child-like tone as she blinked the sleepiness away from her eyes.

Malcolm shook his head. "I would never dream of making fun of you," he said sincerely. "You haven't really slept since Claire was taken, have you?"

She nodded, her lips forming a frown. "I wasn't able to. I guess it just caught up with me."

"Well, we're still waiting on bureaucrats before we can move," he said in irritation. "Catching some sleep might be for the best. It beats the waiting."

"I feel fine now," Elizabeth said stubbornly. "I'm not going to sit on the sidelines while you go and get her back."

Malcolm knew better than to argue with her, even though he thought it was foolish for her to come. "I'm not going to stop you," he said gently as he placed a hand on her shoulder. "But I really think you should stay here with your brother."

Her eyes narrowed dangerously. "I've done enough hiding from my problems these past five years. I used to be a get-my-hands-dirty girl, now I'm a wallflower." His upper lip rose in disgust as she pulled her coat around herself tightly.

"Alright," he said in surrender. "Then let's go wait with Victoria. The search warrant should be coming in soon."

Elizabeth stiffened for a moment before she nodded. "I feel terrible that I'm coming between the two of you."

"Don't be sorry," Malcolm said as he began to walk. "It was my fault for thinking it was a good idea for us to kiss one last time." The memory of her lips against his was still fresh in his mind and the desire to feel her against him again was powerful. He couldn't look at her for fear of making the situation even worse.

"I suppose, it did help me to feel a sense of closure on this mess," Elizabeth said softly. Her footsteps quickened to keep up with his pace. "In that sense, it was a good idea."

"Victoria is right, I should have spoken with her about it first," he replied with a shake of his head. "Sometimes I just move and act without consulting anyone. It's just how I'm used to being. I'm not very good at being in a relationship."

"That's my fault," she said sadly. "You were always amazing with me until I ripped your heart out."

He stopped in front of the open manhole. "Thank you for saying so but it's in the past now. I'm not going to blame you or anyone for my own foolishness."

"She will see that," Elizabeth said encouragingly. "Give her some space and be your charming self and I'm sure she will forgive you."

His lips pulled into a soft smile as he turned his gaze to look upon hers. The way they spoke reminded him of the past and the ability to talk to her about anything. "I'm glad we're friends, Lizzy. I missed being open with you."

"I missed this, too," she said through a smile. "So don't get hurt in there or I will personally drag your ass back out from the depths of hell."

He chuckled as he removed the rest of the

covering from the manhole. "I'll go down first and catch you if you fall," he said teasingly.

"Do you think so little of me?" she asked with a raised brow.

"Well, I'm sure your brother has kept you in a sterile environment," he rationalized. "You must have forgotten what dirt and grime feels like." He nodded sagely, a little too amused with himself.

She wrinkled her nose and pushed past him. "I still know how to get dirty, Malcolm," she said suggestively as she lowered herself into the hole. "I'll go first and help you find the entrance. You always had trouble with that."

"Touché." His lips curled up into a smirk. He watched as she slowly climbed down the ladder into the tunnels of the city. He followed behind her once her head disappeared from sight.

The decent wasn't a very long and the tunnel was lit by lamps along the walls. Wires and pipes stretched on for as far as the eye could see. Malcolm pulled the folded blueprints from his pocket and studied them for a moment to find their bearings.

"We follow these pipes for two hundred feet and then make a right," he said as he glanced up.

Elizabeth chuckled behind him, causing Malcolm to stop and turn around.

"I'm missing something funny?" he asked, his brow arched curiously.

"Nothing," she said, giggling under his gaze.

"I just had an image in my mind of the sperm that made Claire saying the same thing to all his little sperm friends."

Malcolm joined in her laughter, turning away and walking along the wall of the tunnel. "Knowing my sperm, it probably lied in order trick all the others so that it would be first."

"Ohh! That makes sense," Elizabeth said sagely. "She's always pulling little tricks on me."

Malcolm cast his eyes to the floor. "I remember the time she hid one sock from each pair for a week." A sense of nostalgia washed over him, causing a sad smile to form on his lips. "That drove me insane."

Elizabeth continued to giggle as he spoke. "Or the time that she ripped off the labels on all our canned food."

"Oh yes," Malcolm said in a grand voice. "Mystery Meal Month. We actually had some pretty interesting combinations." The stress and anxiety of waiting vanished as they walked and reminisced over fond memories. The past no longer caused him pain, instead he focused on hope for the future.

As they rounded the corner, Victoria came into view. She was sitting down against the wall, typing away at her laptop and speaking to someone through a bluetooth device in her ear.

"Yup, they are here now," she said to the person on the other side of the call. "I'll let them know. Thank you Cam." She tapped a button on the device to hang up the call and closed her laptop. She stood up and placed it in a backpack that was next to her.

"Did my brother have news on when we can go in?" Elizabeth asked, her voice carrying slight anxiousness.

Victoria nodded. "The warrant just arrived. Cameron's team is moving in on the building right now."

"Excellent," Malcolm said happily. "Do you have any idea what's going on in the building?"

"He knows he's being watched by the FBI and assumes Cameron is behind it," Victoria said, her tone all business. "However, he doesn't know about this entrance or our plan to use it. He's mostly worried Malcolm won't surrender and he'll be forced to kill Claire."

"That almost sounds like he cares," Malcolm said bitterly. "Perhaps in a twisted way, he actually does."

Victoria shrugged. "It's strange to listen to him when he thinks no one is listening. He keeps muttering something about *him*."

"I wonder what he means," Elizabeth said thoughtfully. "I seem to recall him being worried about shadow people whenever he visited. I always assumed it had to do with The Organization."

"What did you know about The Organization?" Malcolm asked with an arched brow. "I've been meaning to ask when you learned of it."

Elizabeth laughed. "I always knew about it," she said sweetly. "Who do you think suggested to my father that you be allowed in?"

"I'm not sure if you did me a favor or not," Malcolm grumbled. "I wouldn't be in this mess if not for them."

"It would be worse, I think," Elizabeth replied. "Your only real mistake was ever falling in love and marrying me, Mal. But without the protection of The Organization, my brother would have crushed you before you ever had a chance to fight back."

Malcolm thought about that for a moment and realized that she spoke the truth. "I never thought of it that way before. I've always thought of them as a hassle rather than an asset, but that's mostly because of your brother as well."

"Cameron is giving us the signal," Victoria interjected. "Let's go inside."

Malcolm nodded and watched as she hurried to open the door leading into the maintenance entrance. He could see the pain in her eyes as she struggled to focus on the task at hand and he wanted to comfort her.

"Thank you for being here, Victoria," Elizabeth said softly. "I really hope that you stick around long enough to meet Claire. She spoke really highly of you after she snuck in that phone call to you."

Victoria stopped in her tracks, turning around to face the two of them. Malcolm worried for a moment that all of her pent up rage would explode. Instead, a small smile formed on her lips.

"I would love to," she said fondly. "Just because I'm angry at her daddy doesn't mean she should suffer for it."

"Exactly," Elizabeth agreed. "It would be wrong if we shunned her because we don't like him." She giggled, looking over at Malcolm with a mischievous smile on her lips.

Victoria nodded in agreement. "You're right. It's not her fault that her father is a jerk."

"I'm right here," Malcolm muttered.

The girls chuckled at his response, and said in unison, "We know."

Olivia Noble

Chapter Ten

As the trio passed through the threshold into Brantford's building, they became deathly silent. The echoes of their laughter clung to Victoria's mind and she found herself glancing back at Elizabeth without meaning to. It was surprising to her how well Malcolm's formerly estranged wife had been able to lighten her mood so easily. She was thankful for that and was glad that even though she was angry with Malcolm, that perhaps Elizabeth could be a friend.

Through her earpiece, Victoria could hear Cameron's men presenting the warrant to Brantford's security. They were angry and baffled, but were forced to comply with the search.

"Damn him," she heard Branford hiss into her ear. "Hide her where those idiots won't find her. Why the fuck did my agents not warn me of this?"

She turned to look at Malcolm and Elizabeth

Billionaires Underground

whom were behind her. "He's moving Claire somewhere in the building. The FBI is catching him off guard."

Malcolm nodded. "Do you know where?"

She shook her head. "No, and I don't know where he is either."

"It's a start," he replied. "While we're down here, we should cut the power to the elevators."

Victoria furrowed her brows. "That's a good idea," she said in approval. "Let me see the blueprints."

Malcolm produced them from his jacket and handed them to her. Her eyes scanned over them rapidly until she found what she was looking for. "Alright, I'll go do this. When I hear that Claire is being moved and they are in the elevator, I'll cut the power."

"No," Elizabeth said quickly. "Let me. You two are more capable of dealing with the danger in here and this is something I can do."

Victoria frowned. *Alone*, she thought to herself. It wasn't an idea that she was comfortable with and she wanted to protest. However, she knew that Elizabeth was right. Dragging her into a fight was more likely to get her killed. "Alright," she conceded. "Take this and wait until you hear which floor they are on." Reaching up to her eat, she removed her ear piece and handed the small device to Elizabeth.

"I'll call you once it's done," Elizabeth said

with determination. "Both of you, be careful."

"Always," Malcolm replied through a smile. "Don't be reckless if someone comes down here to fix the problem."

"I should be okay," she said calmly. "Show me where the controls are down here."

Victoria nodded, motioning for Elizabeth to come next to her. "Can you remember this?" she asked in concern.

"Of course," Elizabeth replied sweetly. "I'll let you know when I'm in position. Just put your phones on vibrate."

A slight smile formed on Victoria's lips as she nodded. "We've done this before," she said reassuringly. "We'll be okay."

"Famous last words," Elizabeth countered. "Please bring my baby back safely. I'm sorry I'm not more help."

Victoria shook her head. "Right now, you're being the biggest help I can think of. Malcolm is right though, someone is probably going to come down to fix what you've broken, so be on your guard."

"Stay safe, Lizzy," Malcolm said gently. "We'll bring her back."

It pained Victoria to watch the pair of them embrace but she steeled her heart against it. She turned away from the sight and began walking towards a stairwell. Her hand trembled as it reached out to grasp the metal handle. *Stop it,*

Victoria, she mentally demanded. *I need to focus right now, a little girl depends on it.*

"I'm sorry," said Malcolm's voice gently from behind her.

She spun around to look into his stormy eyes. "For what?" she asked through a forced smile. "You don't have anything to be sorry for."

A flash of pain flew across his eyes and he turned his face away to hide it. "Tell me now if you aren't up for this. I understand."

Her nose wrinkled in frustration. It made her happy that he seemed to care about her but she couldn't get the image out of her mind of his lips locked with another woman's. "I'm hurt by what you did but I'll be fine."

Malcolm studied her for a long moment. She felt hot under his scrutiny and without being able to stop herself, she gently reached out and touched his chest.

"You can count on me," she assured him again.

"I was never concerned with if I could count on you or not," Malcolm said gently, taking her hand into his. "I'm worried that you might get hurt."

"Too late for that," she said softly, pulling her hand away. "I'll be okay. We really need to go."

Malcolm set his jaw as he nodded. "Ladies first," he said, motioning to the door.

She chuckled as brushed passed him. "Stare as much as you can while you can," she said suggestively. "You lost all touching privileges."

"I fully intend on it," Malcolm said, the tension leaving his face. "I think we have something like forty floors to climb."

"Well, at least I won't have to worry about going to the gym for a while," Victoria rationalized. It felt nice to be able to joke with Malcolm. Each laugh and smile numbed the pain in her heart.

"What are your plans for the story after all this?" he asked curiously.

Victoria had a dozen answers she wanted to give him but something in her stopped the words from coming. Joking with him felt awkward enough but sharing her ideas made her stomach lurch. "I'll keep The Organization out of it."

"That's not what I meant," Malcolm said calmly.

"I know but it's the only answer I feel comfortable giving," she said in as even a voice as she could. "Please, cha… Mal, keep this professional." It hurt to push him away when she wanted him close, but he had betrayed her. No justification was ever going to take that away.

"I understand," he said gently. "I didn't mean to upset you."

A bitter response nearly leapt from her tongue. She bit it back, instead forcing out,

"Thanks."

The pair ascended the hostile building in silence. They stopped by each door, cracking it open so that they could listen for any movement. The security was in a rush to move around, trying to stay one step ahead of the FBI that was moving slowly throughout the building.

"We need to climb faster," Malcolm whispered. "I want to get Claire out before any of the fighting begins."

Victoria nodded. "Has Elizabeth tried to contact you?"

He shook his head. "No, and I'm worried."

"About?" she asked with a raised brow.

He hesitated, as if he was struggling with the idea. "That maybe she's not really on our side."

"Oh," she said in surprise. "My instincts tell me she is. She'll call."

He sighed. "I'm going to feel like an idiot when she does, but I can't get over the past so easily."

She placed a gentle hand on his shoulder. "You're doing the best you can, champ. She'll come through." She wanted to comfort him more but this was as much as she could muster while dealing with her own pain.

A soft vibration gently filled the air.

"See?" Victoria said sweetly. "Just be quiet when you pick up."

Malcolm smiled as he reached for his phone.

He hummed lowly in response to the soft voice over the line. The call was short and soon he stuffed the device back in his pocket. "Brantford is ordering his men to lead the FBI into a trap, but she doesn't know the details. Claire is on the thirty second floor, Elizabeth just cut the power to the elevators."

Victoria furrowed his brows. "We need to warn them."

He nodded. "Can you handle that?" he asked, handing her his phone. "It won't be long before the elevators are fixed."

She hesitated. Though she felt uncomfortable with him close, she felt even more uneasy at the idea of being separated. "Yes," she said in a shaky voice, taking his phone and stuffing it into her pocket. "I'll find a way to sneak outside and tell Cameron. Please be careful, champ."

"You too," he said, leaning forward to gently place his lips on her cheek. "We'll all meet in the tunnels."

His footsteps hardly made a sound as he began to quickly climb the stairs alone and Victoria was left with the faint feeling of his touch on her skin. She missed him terribly but forced the feeling away as she opened the door near her.

The floor was empty as far as she knew. Carefully, she navigated through the narrow halls into an office room overlooking the street. Pulling out Malcolm's phone, she slid her thumb across the screen to unlock it and dialed Cameron.

"It's a trap," Victoria said as soon as she heard Cameron picking up.

"Shit," he said. "I'll let me boys know. Where is Claire?"

"Malcolm went to go get her," she explained. "I'm going to go make sure your men don't get killed."

"Don't," Cameron ordered. "They can handle themselves. Just get out of there."

Victoria hung up the phone without answering. She was tired of men telling her what to do. She quickly moved back toward the stairs, slipping into the stairwell quietly. Her feet raced down the stairs towards the sound of voices.

"I hope you are aware of the seriousness of these accusations, sir," a gruff voice said.

"Of course I'm aware, Agent Norton, but the elevators are out of service," a man replied, his voice snakelike and slimy. "If you want to continue your search of the building, you're just going to have to use the stairs."

Victoria's pace quickened and she ducked behind the door, out of sight. The cold wall pressed into her back as she scooted over into the corner. The door in front of her slowly opened, obscuring her from the sight of the two men.

"Right up this way, Agent," the slimy man said. He held the door open for the agent, a creepy smile framed his face.

Olivia Noble

The two men walked past Victoria without seeing her. Norton stood taller than the creepy looking man by at least a foot, and had slicked back brown hair. The security man was slightly heavy set under his suit and his hair was a mess of tight, black curls.

The door behind them closed with an audible clang. Victoria kept herself pressed against the wall, watching the two men ascend slowly. From where she stood, she saw the shorter man reaching into his jacket.

"Watch out!" she shouted.

The men froze momentarily. Norton spun around as the security guard scrambled to finish drawing his gun.

Norton was faster.

In a flash his gun was out and he unloaded three quick shots into the security guard's chest. As the man fell limp against the staircase, Norton turned to look at Victoria.

"Close call," he said nervously.

Victoria sighed. "No kidding. You go upstairs and help Malcolm, I'm going to go find the others."

"Shouldn't that be the other way around?" he asked with a raised brow.

"We really don't have time to argue right now," she said stubbornly. "Go! Thirty second floor."

The agent nodded and began running up the

stairs. "The rest of my men are spread throughout the first few floors…"

"On it," Victoria said as she briskly walked through the door, back into the offices. She knew she needed to move quickly or the unsuspecting agents were going to get slaughtered.

Chapter Eleven

Victoria approached the sound of muffled voices. The walls made it nearly impossible to make out what anyone was saying, but she could gather from the general tone that something violent was about to happen.

Brantford's men patrolled the outside of a corner office. Every one of them had eyes like steel, emotionless and cold. Her fingers traveled her body, searching for the ivory grip of the pistol Malcolm had given her. Slowly, she drew the weapon and held it out in front of her as she walked nearer to her enemies.

Victoria's eyes scanned the hallway, watching carefully for the men's movements. They patrolled in a very lazy way, taking a long walk down the hall, turning the corner and following the office in a giant loop. It was easy for Victoria to simply remain a few steps behind the walking guard. Quickly, she became comfortable in his pattern and the time it took for him to make a full circle. *Two minutes,* she thought to herself.

Without making a sound, she ducked into a cubicle as the man disappeared from sight and set her eyes upon his stationary partner by the door of the office where she could hear the muffled voices. She picked up a stapler from the desk of her hiding place and gently tossed it into an adjoining cubicle. It alerted the door guard and he cautiously approached her hiding spot. Her heart thumped in her chest so loudly she feared it would give her away. Fighting to stay calm, she hid in the darkness as the man scanned the area only a few feet from where she lay.

"Messy people leaving shit where it's not supposed to be," the guard muttered as he turned back toward his post.

One minute, she thought to herself as she dashed out of her hidden place. Taking the gun, she raised it up and struck the guard in the back of the head as hard as she could.

He crumpled in unconsciousness and Victoria caught him before he fell. Slowly, she dragged him to where she was once hidden and stuffed his unconsciousness form under the desk. Then she returned to the darkness, waiting for the patrolling guard to make another circle.

Thirty seconds, she thought as she patiently waited out of sight.

Like clockwork, the patrolling guard turned

the corner and walked at a slow pace toward her. At first, he noticed nothing wrong until he was within line of sight of the door his friend had been guarding.

"Mike?" he called out nervously. "The boss will have your hide if you're taking a piss again." He grumbled to himself and walked past Victoria without noticing her presence.

Again, she lashed out at the passing guard, quickly overtaking him and knocking him unconscious. She stuffed his body next to his comrades' and made her way toward the previously guarded door. Her heard turned to check her surroundings as she cautiously moved closer to her destination.

"What do you think I should do with this one, Jerry?" A woman's voice said, a sick glee resonating in her tone. "Think I should cut on him a little more?"

"Up to you, Becks," the man named Jerry replied, his tone distracted and unamused. "I don't really care what you do with him. Just make sure not to keep all the blood on the tarp."

The woman sighed. "You have no sense of class when it comes to getting information. Do you know that?"

"I just prefer more straight forward methods," he said. "It's like taking out the trash. You don't take pleasure in taking out the trash, you just do it."

"This is why our sex life is miserable," she said in exasperation.

There was the sound of muffled screams echoing through the door. Victoria's blood ran cold at the sound, a shiver crawling up her spine. She poked her head into the room, seeing the raven-haired interrogator and her tall companion.

"Tell me," the raven-haired woman said slowly, her voice filled with honey. "How did you plan on getting out of here alive? Surely you at the FBI know who you are dealing with here."

Victoria watched in horror as the woman slowly sank her knife into the agent's shoulder. He screamed out in pain, even as his torturer whispered sweetly to him.

"Did you really think you could flash your silly little badges and get the girl we've spent so much time keeping hidden away? Did you really think you could take her back to her father so easily?" She twisted the blade, causing another muffled shriek of pain from the agent. "Your partner is probably dead by now. All of your friends soon will be but you have a chance to go see your family again. Would you like that? Would you like me to make all this pain stop?"

Victoria couldn't stand by any longer. As the woman removed the gag from the agent's mouth, Victoria dived into the room with her weapon drawn. Without hesitation she fired three rounds at the man who was standing next to the raven-haired women. The sound of the impact was thick, as if it ran into something hard rather than flesh. *A vest,* Victoria quickly surmised.

"Jerry!" the woman shrieked, turning to face Victoria with hate burning in her eyes.

Her hand reached for her own weapon but Victoria was faster, shooting another round that nicked the woman's face. She howled in pain as her body spun around as if trying to avoid the damage that had already been inflicted.

"Where are the others?" Victoria demanded, keeping her pistol aimed at the raven-haired woman.

"Probably dead or in a similar state as this one," the woman hissed. "Like you soon will be."

Victoria guessed that the woman was also wearing a vest and squeezed the trigger, aiming at center mass. There was a similar sound as the bullet impacted her chest. She fell to the ground, groaning in pain.

"I'm not going to play a game with you," Victoria said slowly. "You either tell me what I want to know by the count of three or I make sure you aren't recognizable at your funeral. Then I do the same to your boy-toy." She couldn't believe the words that were coming out of her mouth or the way her life had changed since meeting Malcolm. However, something about the woman before Victoria was so appalling that she almost felt it would be a public service to kill her. Only her sense of compassion stayed her hand.

"I have nothing to say to you," the woman groaned.

"One," Victoria said seriously.

The woman said nothing, just looked at Victoria with eyes of rage.

"Two," Victoria continued.

The man flinched, coming to his senses. Victoria caught it out of the corner of her eye and ducked as the man reached for his weapon, firing in her general direction. Grunting in frustration, Victoria peeked out from behind the desk that was acting as cover. A bullet screamed past her face, the raven-haired woman missing by only a hairsbreadth.

"Three," Victoria said as she pulled the trigger, hitting the woman square in the forehead.

"Becks!" The man cried out mournfully. He aimed his weapon at Victoria and squeezed the trigger.

She had no time to react. The world was in slow motion and when the sound of the shot came, she jumped reflexively. Pain that she had expected never came. Her hands touched her body in disbelief but found nothing wrong. She looked back toward the man that she was sure had killed her and saw him lying limp on the floor.

The agent was standing up, blood running down his shoulder in tiny steams. His body was pale from the loss of blood and he soon stumbled back, catching himself on the wall only barely.

"We need to get you out of here," Victoria said in concern.

The agent shook his head. "My partner," he gasped out.

"He's fine. I already saved him," she said soothingly. "I expect both of you boys to treat me to a drink." She was trying to lighten the mood and give him something to look forward to.

When she saw his lips pull into a faint smile, she joined him with one of her own.

"I think I might owe you two," he said lightheartedly even as he bled.

Victoria walked over to him briskly, offering him her shoulder as support. "The elevators are out, so we're going to have to take the stairs. Be tough."

The agent nodded. "I'll try."

Chapter Twelve

Malcolm's stormy eyes scanned the thirty second floor from the staircase door. It was mostly filled with cubicles and was dimly lit. Someone could easily be awaiting him in ambush. *Damn,* he mentally cursed. His nose wrinkled in frustration at the situation. He knew he had no choice but to proceed through dangerous enemy territory if he wanted to reach the elevators on the other side of the room.

He closed the door behind him carefully, as if not to make a sound. His steps were quiet as he made his way into the main office floor. Every sense was on alert for the slightest hint of movement or danger. The hairs on his arms and neck stood on end and his mouth felt like a desert. From where he stood, he could see the elevator corridor where his daughter was trapped. *I'm almost there, Claire.*

A shadow of movement caught Malcolm's

keen eyes. His feet came to a sudden halt as he gazed in the direction of the offending space. Narrowing his eyes, Malcolm lashed out with his foot, kicking the wall of the cubicle down, breaking it at the seams. A grunt revealed a person under the wall. Malcolm approached with caution, his gun drawn and out in front of him. Lifting the rubble off the man, he was met with the cold gaze of his worst enemy.

"Hello," Malcolm said calmly, his eyes dancing with determination. "Brantford."

His enemy's face contorted into hate and rage. "Do it," he hissed.

Malcolm could feel the pressure of his finger against the trigger and wanted to squeeze so badly. "Stand up," he ordered. "I'm not going to end it between us like this."

"Oh?" Brantford asked contemptuously. "The dog has honor? Spare me the sentiment and just end it."

"We were brothers once," Malcolm replied, ignoring the insult. "We'll end this like men. Now get up or are you just that eager to die?"

Brantford seemed to think the idea over in his head. Finally, he slowly began to stand up. "You should have killed me when you had the chance, dog."

"I wish it hadn't come to this, Brantford," Malcolm said sadly. "This is only going to hurt the people we care about."

Brantford shrugged his shoulders. "That's life."

A deep sigh escaped Malcolm's throat as he kept his gun pointed ahead. "Put the gun you have on that shoulder strap down and the knife stuffed in your sock. Also the shitty thirty eight stuffed behind your waist."

"Nothing escapes the great Malcolm Cage, does it?" Brantford asked sardonically. "I suppose it's fitting for an animal to want to finish this with his bare hands."

"You made this personal," Malcolm reminded him. "So we're going to end it ourselves."

Brantford wrinkled his nose in disgust as he slowly reached for his gun. Making no sudden movements, he drew it from his holster, the gun hanging upside down on his finger. He tossed it aside and reached for the small thirty-eight revolver from behind his waist, discarding it the same way. With a sigh, he lifted his foot and slid his sock down far enough to reveal the razor sharp knife. He tossed it away near the pile of his other weapons and looked at Malcolm expectantly.

"Now back away," Malcolm ordered, keeping his gun pointed at his enemy.

The two of them walked deeper into the office, away from the weapons. Once Malcolm was satisfied, he put his gun on safety and tossed it away as well. They exchanged hate filled glances for a moment before Malcolm folded his hands out in front of him. He bowed respectfully, keeping his eyes on his enemy the entire time.

Brantford set his jaw in anger, clearly repulsed by the idea of showing Malcolm respect. After a moment of struggling with his pride, he also bows and the pair of them step back into fighting position. Calmly, Malcolm scanned the area around him. *Five feet of movement in all directions. Three feet between Brantford and me. Twenty feet from his weapons.*

While he analyzed the room, Brantford made the first move, stepping quickly to close the distance between them. He lashed out with violent and quick strikes that Malcolm parried away smoothly. His enemy was skilled and moved with the power and grace of a tiger. Malcolm felt himself pushed back, toward the weapons that had been discarded.

Sidestepping a powerful punch, Malcolm grasped Brantford's side, violently throwing him to the ground in a single, smooth motion. As Brantford fell, he pulled Malcolm with him and the pair struggled to gain an advantage on the ground.

It happened so fast that Malcolm wasn't able to respond. Brantford snaked his arm around Malcolm's neck and squeezed until his air was cut off, making it difficult to breathe. His fingers gripped Brantford's arm as he tried to pry away his hold.

"I told you that you should have killed me when you had the chance!" Brantford cried out victoriously as he squeezed even harder.

The world was starting to become black. It was impossible to breath and it felt like his neck was close to snapping. In a violent effort, Malcolm threw himself backward, taking both of them off balance. Life came rushing back into his lungs as he gasped for air. His vision was still blurry and he couldn't see Brantford striking him hard across the face with a keyboard.

The impact sent him reeling as the sound of scattered, breaking plastic filled the air. Blood filled his mouth, overwhelming him with a potent metallic taste. He rolled away, creating space between the two of them, and allowing himself a moment to recover.

Brantford took the opportunity to move towards his discarded weapons. Malcolm had allowed them to get to close to the firearms and he dived behind a cubicle to stay hidden.

"Come out, Mal," Brantford said in a tone filled with delight. He fired off a shot toward Malcolm's direction, laughing as he did so.

"I never could understand the pleasure you took in other people's pain," Malcolm said from where he was hidden.

"That's the world we live in, Mal," Brantford replied. "You're either the wolf or the sheep."

Malcolm sighed and scanned the room for

the place he had discarded his own weapon. "That's not all it is," he said as he inched closer. "You take pleasure in hurting your own family. Your sister, your brother and my niece, all of them want to love you, but all you do is hurt them."

Brantford growled in rage and fired off several more rounds. "Come out!" he demanded. "Shut up you fucking mutt."

A bullet ripped through the wall in front of Malcolm. He froze in place. *Six shots left and another six in his thirty eight,* he mentally calculated. He quietly crawled his way toward his gun, moving as quickly as he could.

"What, no more remarks? Or did I kill you already?" Brantford asked, fury in his voice.

The smooth ivory grip felt good against Malcolm's fingers as he grasped his custom colt. He stood quickly and fired three rapid shots, using Brantford's voice as his guide. His enemy crumpled to the floor, crying out in agony. Cautiously, Malcolm approached his fallen adversary with his gun held firmly out in front of him.

The sight of Brantford's body, bloodied with three wounds in his chest, was almost more than Malcolm could bear.

"Ha," Brantford croaked out. "I suppose a… congratulations… is in order."

"Don't talk," Malcolm said soothingly, kneeling down beside the dying man. "Do you want me to call Elizabeth and Cameron so that they can say goodbye?"

Brantford shook his head. "You have to promise me something… mutt."

"What?" Malcolm asked curiously.

"You have to protect them from what's coming next," Brantford said, his breathing labored and coming out in short, awful gasps.

"What do you mean?" Malcolm asked, his brow rising suspiciously.

Brantford reached out and grabbed Malcolm's arm in a vice grip. "Look… to… your… past." The words were forced out, as if he was living on sheer willpower. "Promise me."

"Of course I promise," Malcolm said with fierce determination. "You have my word they will be safe."

"Good," he gasped as the life flowed out of him.

Malcolm stood above the body of someone he used to call *brother,* and felt the stinging of tears in the corner of his eyes. "You stubborn fool," he hissed. "You bloody stubborn fool." With a shaky breath, Malcolm stood. He leaned against the wall of a cubicle for a moment, gathering himself and coming to terms with what he had to do.

Olivia Noble

Chapter Thirteen

Elizabeth wept, though she was unsure why. Was it because her brother was dead and she mourned him or was it because her brother was dead and she felt safe? The thought haunted her mind, only making her sobs increase in frequency and strength. Everything could be heard through the listening device hooked up to Brantford's phone. The horrible fight and the shooting sounded so close, she almost felt as if she was there.

Even at the end, Malcolm comforted his enemy and promised him that he would keep his family safe. It was too much for her to bear and her emotions spilled out in the privacy of the building's lonely basement. She would have fixed the elevators, but she quickly learned it was far easier to break them than it was to get them back in working order. *I need to go up and help him*, she thought to herself. Now that her brother was dead, she figured it would be safe for her to make her way into the building unescorted.

Movement at the exit caught her attention. It was far away and she couldn't quite make out who it was in the dim lighting but she could clearly see that it was a woman's form. Victoria came to mind but there was something different about the way this person moved. Elizabeth watched the unknown female carefully, her hand gripping the gun she had borrowed from Malcolm's armory.

The woman glanced around, unsure of her surroundings at first. Clearly, she had never been to this part of the building. "Yeah, I'm down here. No fucking idea where the controls are though," she said in an irritated voice to an unseen party. "On the back left wall? Alright, I'm heading over there."

Sweat formed on Elizabeth's brow as she maneuvered herself to stay out of sight. Was this person a friend or foe? She wasn't sure and didn't want to take the risk of finding out. The woman briskly walked over to where Elizabeth had been, her heels clicking and echoing in the room.

"Jesus, what a mess," the woman said.

Being so close, Elizabeth could see the woman had deep red hair tied up into a tight bun. She watched the red head try to fix the damage she had caused to the circuits controlling the various parts of the building. Frustration was clearly growing in the woman as she threw her arms up in disbelief.

"I'm not an electrician, Mack," the woman said. "This is horse shit. Someone clearly broke it. The boss is going to be pissed if we can't move the girl."

That confirmed Elizabeth's suspicions and she drew her weapon slowly. "Hands up," she said fiercely.

The woman turned around sharply, reaching for her own weapon out of instinct. "Who are you?"

"Your boss... my brother is dead," Elizabeth replied, her voice wracked with pain. "Just drop your weapon."

"Not going to happen, blondie," the woman said, her eyes narrowing. "Brantford isn't dead. You're fucking with me."

Elizabeth shook her head. "Honestly, I don't know if I wished I was. My husband just won this stupid fucking game and we want our daughter back."

"Your husband?" the woman asked, rage building in her voice. "You just said you're the boss' sister and you're married to the guy that you say killed him?" She broke out in laughter. "Honey, I think you're insane. Malcolm Cage," she spat the name. "Would never win against the boss. He's been chasing his own tail for years."

"*Listen*," Elizabeth hissed. "I don't care what you believe, but you need to put your gun down and walk away. There's been enough violence already."

The woman laughed again. "I don't think you even have the stones to pull the trigger. Look at you," she said mockingly. "You look like you belong at a tea party."

Elizabeth wrinkled her nose in frustration. She hated that description of herself. Malcolm had always loved her tomboyish nature, but Brantford would constantly put her down for it. Five years with him had almost completely driven out any remnant of the old girl she used to be. "I won't ask you again. I just want my daughter."

The woman's eyes went wide in shock. "What?!" she screeched. "You're fucking kidding me. The boss really got wacked?" She looked at Elizabeth, her eyes suddenly filling up with hate as she reached for her weapon.

Elizabeth felt her body freeze up as she saw the cold metal pointed at her. She tried to will herself to shoot but nothing happened. Sudden pain filled her entire body as a bullet connected with her vest, right over her heart. She collapsed onto the ground, feeling as if she couldn't breathe.

"I'm going to kill you and then your little girl and your husband," the red head said venomously. "No, Mack, I'm not going to fucking stand down. These pricks killed the boss."

More tears welled up in her eyes. Some were from emotion but mostly the pain. She looked up into the fury of the woman's eyes. "Did he mean something to you?" she asked in a shaky voice.

The red head hesitated. "None of your business."

"He was my brother," Elizabeth replied sadly. "I know how you feel."

"If he was your brother, you should have killed your husband!" the woman demanded, pointing her gun at Elizabeth's face. "You should have had his back."

A deep frown formed on Elizabeth's face. "I loved my brother but he threatened my daughter. That's a mistake both of you made." She squeezed the trigger of her gun and felt the powerful recoil push her back against the hard concrete. Blood splatter hit her in the face and stained her clothes red. She lie there for a moment, struggling to breathe from the pain in her chest. Slowly, she stood up and saw the red haired woman dead on the ground. *It's all so fucking senseless*, she agonized mentally.

There was no time to be emotional; if others reacted this way to the news of Brantford's death, there was no telling what kind of danger her family was really in. She couldn't be here anymore. As quickly as she was able, Elizabeth walked toward the door leading to the stairs. The metal creaked open as she approached. The temptation to dive out of sight was overridden by the pain shooting through her body as soon as she tried to make the sudden movement.

"What the hell happened here?" the familiar sound of Victoria's voice reverberated in the basement. "Elizabeth, are you okay?"

Elizabeth clutched at her chest. "If getting shot in the boob through a vest doesn't count. Yes, I'm perfectly fine."

Victoria's lips pulled into a tight frown. She glanced around and saw the dead woman across the room. "I'm sorry I wasn't here to back you up."

"I handled myself as well as I could," she replied, forcing herself to smile. "If it's all the same to you, let's please just go get my daughter."

"Right."

Malcolm approached the elevator door with caution. "Claire," he said loudly.

"Daddy!" The sound of her innocent voice was muffled by the walls.

"Are you alright, princess?" he asked, feeling relief wash over him.

"Yes," she said through the door. "Mr. Philips has been nice and telling me stories."

Malcolm's brow rose. "I'm going to get you

out of there," he said. "Mr. Philips, whoever you are, don't make this harder."

"I have no intentions of doing so," the man said calmly.

There was a strange familiarity about the man's voice that he couldn't quite put his finger on. Putting it out of his mind, Malcolm pried open the elevator door with a screw driver he had found in one of the desks. The length of the metal bar made it difficult to wedge the door open, but finally he was able to pull it apart wide enough so that he could use his fingers. He pulled the first set of doors open, and repeated the same motions with the doors of the elevator car. As they slid open, Claire's form was revealed to him and she quickly pounced him.

"Daddy!" she shouted, wrapping her arms around his neck.

"Oh princess," he said softly, tears flowing down his eyes. "I've missed you so much."

"I'm so sorry we left you alone," Claire said, burying her head into his shoulder. "You must have been so lonely."

"It doesn't matter anymore sweetheart. Being able to hug you now is all that matters." His eyes looked at the unknown man who stood there silently. Malcolm took note of his greying hair and piercing grey eyes. "You don't look like one of Brantford's men."

"And just what does one of Mr.

Cunningham's men look like?" The older man asked in an amused tone. "Do they just have a look about them I'm not aware of?"

Malcolm felt irritation building and forced it out with a deep breath. "I'll rephrase. Who are you?"

"The man Mr. Cunningham entrusted with your daughter's care while the two of you... exchanged words," Mr. Philips said calmly. "Now that this ugly business has been concluded, I have further instructions." He slowly reached into his jacket and produced a small USB stick. "This is for you, Mr. Cage. It contains important information you will need to handle Mr. Cunningham's estate and much more."

"Forgive me for being skeptical, but I feel this is all a bit too convenient," Malcolm said dubiously. Brantford's words echoed in his mind, *look into your past.* What did it mean, and was the information on the USB a clue?

Philips shrugged. "It's not my concern any longer. I'm only here to help facilitate the ending of this conflict."

Malcolm knew that this man must somehow be with the Organization but he had no idea who this man really was. "Thank you," he said as he reached out to accept the small device.

"Of course, Mr. Cage. Good day to you," he said pleasantly. His eyes looked upon Claire for a moment, fondness flashing across them. "I hope to see you again, little one. It's been a pleasure to meet you."

Claire had remained silent this entire time, long ago learning to pay close attention when the adults were speaking. "You tell the best stories," she said brightly. "Thank you for keeping me company."

"Any time," he said through a smile. He walked through the elevator door, turned and headed toward the stairs.

"Daddy," Claire asked sweetly. "Where is Uncle Brant?"

Malcolm felt a pang of regret stabbing through his heart. "He's sleeping, dear one."

"I'll miss him," she said sadly. "He could be mean and frightening, but I think he was a good person deep down."

The insight of her words made his chest swell with pride and his heart break at the same time. "Never change, Claire," he said softly. "Let's go find your mother."

Chapter Fourteen

Claire's weight was comfortable in Malcolm's arms as he walked down the stairs. Being able to feel her, to smell her hair and listen to her voice made his heart sore to the moon. He had his little girl back and nothing else mattered anymore.

"I can walk," she said in a playfully grumpy voice.

"I know, but I miss carrying you," he said fondly. "Though I don't remember you being quite so heavy."

She wrinkled her, making her face look adorably angry. "That's what happens when a girl grows up," she proclaimed. "And because you teased me, I demand ice cream."

"Is that in some rule book I wasn't aware of?" He asked with a raised brow.

"It is now," she said, her lips pulling into a smile. She leaned in and kissed her father on the cheek.

He felt the muscles in his jaw ache from smiling too much. His fingers ruffled the top of her head and pressed his forehead against hers. "Well, I suppose you can have some ice cream on the way home."

She giggled lightly, the sound echoing in the stairwell like the chime of the sweetest bells. He felt his foot connect with solid ground as he stepped off the stairs. They had covered a little over thirty floors in order to get to the lobby and it almost felt too good to be true. All he had to do was open this final door and he was that much closer to exiting the building and getting back to his life.

He pushed the door open and his eyes were greeted with the sight of Elizabeth and Victoria briskly walking across the floor toward them. The pair of them stopped in their tracks. Elizabeth's eyes went wide and tears glistened from a distance.

"Oh my baby," she gasped as she took off into a run toward them.

"Mommy!" the little girl shouted excitedly.

Malcolm outstretched his free arm to hold her tightly in an embrace with their daughter. It was hard to believe what they had been through, even though Malcolm had been there to experience it all.

"Mal," she sniffled. "Thank you so much. You brought her back to me."

"I always will," he said softly, his own tears beginning to overtake him. "Claire, there is someone I would like you to meet," he announced. Malcolm gently set his daughter down and missed her weight against him. "This is Victoria."

Claire's eyes followed her father's arm and her lips broke out into a wide smile as she looked upon Victoria for the first time. "You're the woman I talked to on the phone. The one who saved my dad."

"That's right," Victoria said, her voice choked up. "I'm glad that I could help your family find you."

Claire walked over to her and without warning, threw her little arms around Victoria's waist. "Thank you," she said quietly.

Victoria looked shocked for a moment before she awkwardly hugged the little girl back. "You are more than welcome," she replied fondly, stroking the girl's back as lovingly as any mother.

The sight was more than Malcolm could deal with. An emotional dam was broken and he allowed himself to cry openly in front of the people he considered family. "I'm the happiest man on earth right now."

Elizabeth smiled and linked her arm with his. "That makes two of us. Except without being the man part. You can keep that."

He laughed lightly in his throat. "I intend on it." He looked over at Victoria to see that her lips formed a slight frown. "If you ladies will excuse me, I'd like to have a word with Victoria."

"Okay," Claire grumbled as she unfolded her arms from the woman. "I like her, dad."

"I like her, too," he replied, keeping his eyes on the woman he loved.

Her cheeks became slightly darker as she blushed and she averted her eyes from Malcolm's intense gaze. "Are you sure?" she asked defensively. "Maybe you should just spend the time with your daughter."

"It's okay!" Claire interjected. "I've missed him for years now. A few more minutes isn't going to kill me."

Malcolm was glad to see that his daughter had matured so well in the years that he was away. It made him happy to know that his choice in woman was wise. "It'll only take a moment," he assured Victoria. He stepped away from his family and walked towards Victoria with purpose and passion in each stride.

Elizabeth took Claire by the hand and led her away, toward the lobby door where Cameron was waiting for them. Several agents were all around placing members of Brantford's security under arrest.

"So," Victoria said nervously. "What do you want to talk about?"

"Us," he said softly. "I said I wanted to when this was all over and now it is. My daughter is safe and we can go back to our lives. I want you to be there with me."

"You have your wife and little girl back, Malcolm," she said dismissively. "You don't need me anymore."

He sighed and reached out to take her hands in his. She recoiled away, shaking her head softly.

"This was never about replacing Elizabeth, Victoria," he said sincerely. "What we have is real. I know what I did hurt you and I understand that you want to walk away, but you shouldn't."

Victoria looked at her feet, the gears turning in her mind. "You aren't making this very easy. Just be a jerk or something."

A lighthearted laugh escaped from Malcolm's chest. "I've already been a jerk. I thought I'd give being nice a try."

Her lips formed a smile as she looked back up at him. "I appreciate you being understanding. However, I can't ever forget what I saw," she said sadly. "It wasn't that you kissed her, Mal. It was that you kissed her without ever talking to me about it first and the way you kissed her. I think that if I hadn't walked in when I did, you'd have ripped her clothes off and Claire would stop being an only child."

Malcolm frowned, a feeling of shame welling up in his heart. He just wasn't sure if it was because Victoria was wrong, or if it was because she was right. "When you put it like that, it leaves me at a loss for words. I treasure you, Victoria. I can't stand the idea of this relationship ending. Not when we finally earned a chance to really be in it."

"I look at it like I had a billionaire phase. You had a young reporter phase and now we should just go our separate ways," she said, her voice getting colder with each word. "I'm sorry, Malcolm. I know that's a mean thing to say and I don't want to hurt you. It's just how I have to think about this in order to deal with the hurt."

As much as her words pained his ego and his heart, he respected her for them. "Thank you for telling me how you feel," he said somberly. "You're truly an amazing woman, Victoria Chase. I love you."

A tear formed in her eye that she quickly brushed away. "I love you, too. But there are two people who love and need you a whole lot more than I do."

He glanced over at Elizabeth and Claire, standing patiently for him by the exit of the building. His daughter saw that he was looking and waved happily toward him, her innocent face painted with a large grin. He smiled back at her before returning his gaze to Victoria.

"I need you," he said seriously, taking a step closer to her and wrapping his arms around her waist.

"What are you…" she tried to say but was cut off by Malcolm's lips pressing against hers.

She fought against him for a moment before her body succumbed to his advances. She kissed him back with passion, her hands gripping into his shoulders and pulling him closer.

"You are and will always be my choice, my treasure." His voice was throaty and breathless. "Don't walk away from this."

Her face was flush as she looked up at him. "I'll... I'll think about it," she said hesitantly. "I need some time."

"Take all the time you need," he replied gently. "I have a question for you."

"More?" she asked teasingly.

His lips pulled into a tight, friendly smile as he nodded. "Would you go see a movie with us?"

"But Mal," she said in surprise. "That's your thing with Claire."

"I know and I would be honored if you joined us," he said gently. "No matter what happens between you and I, you're still family."

A soft smile crossed Victoria's face. "Not this time. Go take your daughter and Elizabeth out. I'll happily take a rain check," she said, her voice filled with bittersweet fondness. "I just think that time has been frozen for the three of you since that night and you need to restart it together."

He frowned slightly, nodding his head in understanding. "I'll cash in on that check."

"Good," she said, her lips pulling into a smile. She gently placed her hand on Malcolm's arm. "Now go be with your family."

Chapter Fifteen

Victoria lightly traced her lips with the tip of her finger. She missed Malcolm's lips against hers and she fought hard against the temptation to run after him. As much as it hurt her now, she had to believe it was the right thing to do. He was going to be with his family and take care of them. *I'll be fine* she mentally encouraged herself.

Turning on her heel, she watched as Malcolm handed off a small device to Cameron and then get into a car with his daughter and Elizabeth. The pangs of loneliness were already starting to ingrain themselves inside her heart and she forced herself to steel the fragile organ.

"You don't look so well," Cameron said gently as he approached her.

"I'm as fine as I can be," she replied through a forced smile. "I'm just glad we won. How are you men?"

Cameron's eyes flashed anger for a split

second before he regained his natural composure. "Roughed up, but alive thanks to you."

That was good news that she could smile about. "I'm so glad," she said sincerely. "I was worried I didn't get to them in time."

"You did and they have you to thank for their lives," he said as he gently placed a hand on her shoulder. "For a reporter, you did well."

Her brows furrowed in irritation. "Well, for a glorified cop, you didn't do too badly yourself."

A lighthearted chuckle escaped his throat. "It's almost a shame that the real truth of this can't ever make the headlines."

Disgust welled up in her chest as she nodded in agreement. "I'll be damned if some of this isn't out there. The public has a right to know that Brantford Cunningham was a true bastard. It's not like I can prove much of anything else."

Cameron wrinkled his nose. "Soon, the laundry will be done and no one will be the wiser to any of the stains."

"Is that how you people view this kind of thing?" she asked coldly. "Just like taking out the garbage or doing chores. People died today… I killed someone."

Cameron's full lips formed a deep frown. "I know," he said solemnly. "My brother was one of them."

Her cheeks flushed in shame and she averted her eyes from his. "I'm sorry, I didn't mean…"

"Don't worry about it," he said, waving his hand dismissively. "To answer your question… sometimes. The world is an ugly place and it's the most ugly where people have the most to gain or lose. Either the mess is cleaned up or it taints everything else."

"I wonder if it wouldn't be better that way," Victoria said, sighing in agitation. "It's my job to report the truth, not hide it."

"I think the best reporters know when to reveal the truth and when not to," he said reassuringly. "It's a powerful weapon that must be wielded properly."

She placed her palm against her forehead as she nodded. "I understand, it's just frustrating."

"Think of it this way, you have more than enough proof to clear Malcolm's name," he said through a small smile.

"Which I will do first thing as soon as I get home," she said in agreement. "Well, I'll shower first. I feel like I'm covered in blood and brain again."

"You are," Cameron replied soberly. "Just a little."

Victoria rolled her eyes even as her lips formed a tight lipped smile. "I'll miss you, Cam."

"I wouldn't count on me being a total stranger," he said gently. "I'll be around."

His assurance made her feel far better than she had expected. Her arms naturally pulled him into a hug, her head resting against his chest. "Take care of yourself, Cam."

"I always do," he replied, his voice carrying a mirthful tone. "I'll give you a ride back to your apartment?"

She thought about his request for a moment. There was dried blood she could feel becoming caked onto her body and clothes, making her feel disgusting. She could only imagine how bad it looked from another's point of view. "I think that would be for the best," she said, wrinkling her nose. "Someone might think I'm a mass murderer otherwise."

Elizabeth had never had blood on her before. When it dried it became unbearably itchy on her skin and the very thought that it used to be inside another person disgusted her. The smell of it was revolting and made her gag if she breathed in too deeply. When Malcolm suggested the three of them go see a movie at the drive-in theater, she was thrilled, but first she needed to shower.

The long drive out of the city to Malcolm's home had only made the feeling of blood worsen.

She hardly had time to enjoy Claire's enthusiastic reaction to being with her family again. Her feet carried her to the shower as quickly as they could and she felt at ease knowing the strongest man in the world was looking after her daughter. It allowed her to actually enjoy the cascading water over her body. Each moment that passed made her feel more and more relaxed and at ease. Even the strange handing off of information to her brother was only a minor distraction from the warmth of the steam shower.

She wanted to stay under the water for hours and she knew it was possible with the way the water was heated. No matter how much soap she used or how hard she scrubbed, the feeling of a person's soul was impossible to wash away. *I can't hide in here forever*, she thought to herself sadly. Her fingers gripped the faucet and she slowly turned the shower off. Not wanting to keep her family waiting longer than they needed to, she quickly stepped out and dried herself off. The only problem was with her hair, so she abandoned the idea of styling it once it was dry, instead putting it into a simple ponytail.

A black vest, white t-shirt and comfortable blue jeans waited for her as she stepped back into the room. Malcolm had set them out and his thoughtfulness brought a smile to her lips. She put on the casual wear, glad to be in something other than fine cloth. It made her feel normal and young even though she was nearing her mid-thirties. The thought of her age made her nose wrinkle.

"Alright, I'm ready," she called down the stairs as she finished putting on her clothes.

"Hurry up, Mommy, we're going to be late!" Claire exclaimed.

"Darling, your father owns the movie theater," Elizabeth reminded her gently as she walked down the steps. "I don't think we can be late."

Claire flashed her a toothy smile. "Still," she said professionally. "You should always be early."

"Hmm, that's good advice," Elizabeth agreed. "I wonder who taught you that."

"I'm sure *you* did," Malcolm interjected. "Because I know for a fact that I've never heard the meaning of the word. My motto is, *keep them waiting, you're more important than they are.*"

Elizabeth raised a brow. "Don't go teaching her those arrogant habits."

Malcolm winked at her. "Ice cream is good for her and public schools are the way to go," he said sagely.

For the briefest of moments, she regretted reuniting Claire with her father. "Darling, listen to nothing this man says," she commanded.

"Yes mother," Claire said, her lips pulled into a wide smile.

"I do believe I'm getting ganged up on," Malcolm said with mock hurt. "I can't win against you beautiful ladies."

A flush of red invaded Elizabeth's cheeks. Even though she knew his heart belonged to another, she couldn't help but feel flattered by his words. "Good," she said stiffly. "As long as you understand."

Malcolm chuckled. "Since your mother is finally ready, shall we go?"

"Yes!" Claire exclaimed, hugging her father before they walked out of the door.

It was like looking back in time. Five years apart had done nothing to the relationship between father and daughter. They were still as close and Elizabeth remembered, but this time she didn't feel so much on the outside. She was finally able to follow them to their private bonding moment, just as she had wanted to do on that dreadful day. A cold sweat suddenly appeared on her brow as the memory of Brantford's threatening voice echoed in her mind. Her breathing quickened and her chest tightened to the point of pain. Hands searched frantically for something to grab onto, she felt as if she would collapse.

"Relax," a strong voice said soothingly. "Just breathe," it ordered.

Powerful arms steadied her and pulled her back into reality. Her eyes strained to comprehend what they saw, light pained her and sounds were garbled up into incoherent noises. She felt herself being lifted off of the ground and held tightly against something both hard and soft at the same time. She searched the room for what it could be until her eyes fell onto the piercing dark orbs of her husband.

"Mal?" she asked breathlessly.

"It's okay," he said softly. "You're okay."

Her head nodded without her realizing it. His voice and closeness made her anxiety slowly evaporate.

"Mommy," a tiny voice said.

Elizabeth searched for the voice. She saw her daughter's radiant face twisted up into fear.

"I'm okay, darling," she said with forced calmness. "Just got a little dizzy is all."

"Your mother will be fine," Malcolm echoed. "Go wait in the car, princess."

"Yes sir," she said, seemingly feeling better.

Elizabeth's lips pulled into a deep frown. "God, I'm ruining this for you two," she said shamefully. "Just go. I'll stay here."

"Not a chance in hell," Malcolm said fondly. "It was always a mistake to go with her alone. I was being selfish because to two of you always had one another while I worked. Knowing you were taken from me the day you decided to join Claire and me in our time together was the most heartbreaking thing I could imagine. I'll be damned to hell if I let you miss another movie date."

"Mal," she said in a shaking voice. "I love

you." tears formed in her eyes that she couldn't control. His eyes and voice penetrated her very soul and she felt as light as a feather and heavy as brick all at once.

"I love you, too," he said gently. "And even though I'm not putting my penis inside you anymore, we're always family."

"Oh god," Elizabeth said, unable to stop the laughter that tore through her lungs. "I'm glad Claire couldn't hear that."

Malcolm flashed her a broad, boyish grin. "Feeling better now?" he asked gently.

"I am," she said truthfully. The absurdness of his statement made her anxiety vanish. "Thank you, for being you."

He pulled her tightly against his chest, gently kissing her brow. "Anytime."

She set her down with such care, it made her feel as if she were precious cargo. It sent a thrill up her spine and her face flushed in excitement. "I think I've made the two of you wait long enough. Five years is a long time. Shall we go?"

"I would love to."

Chapter Sixteen

Claire had fallen asleep and lay nestled between her parents, snoozing peacefully throughout most of the movie. As the credits appeared on the large projection screen, Elizabeth was left with a sense of satisfaction and gently pulled her daughter closer. She turned to look at the man she had married and felt her lips pull into a tight, private smile. It had amazed her that he remembered the movie they were supposed to see that night and he had surprised them it.

The only thing that was different was his car. He no longer drove the old beat up Ford GT, but now a large SUV that he claimed made him feel more comfortable driving them in during the winter.

"It really does feel like that the danger is over," she said softly as to not wake her sleeping daughter.

Malcolm met her gaze and nodded gently.

"I'm glad that it is," he whispered. "It feels like it has been five years since you walked into my building and I can almost forget the pain of you being gone at all."

"It has certainly felt like several lifetimes have passed," she agreed. "I'm sorry that Victoria wasn't here with us. I would have liked her to have been."

His features softened into near sadness. "She's understandably upset," he said, forcing his lips to smile. "But it was really wonderful to be able to do this with you and Claire as a family. I think she was looking out for us in a way."

Elizabeth shook her head. "I need to have a talk with her," she said firmly. "Sacrifice sounds all noble on the surface, but she should really be more worried about her own happiness."

His brows furrowed as she spoke. "You mean, you're really going to support her being with me? I suppose I'm surprised at how mature the two of you are being."

Elizabeth stifled a laugh. "Oh, honey," she said, her voice dripping with sweetness. "I never said anything about being okay with it."

"What are you saying, Lizzy?" he asked, his voice sounding strained.

"Victoria loves you but I do as well," she said seriously. "I'm saying that even though I love you and want to renew our vows, I'm not going to let Victoria make the same mistake I did." She

Olivia Noble

gently reached over and brushed the tips of her fingers across his chin. "What's important is that we will be friends no matter what."

"Thank you, Lizzy," he said quietly. "Other than the munchkin, that's what I've missed the most these past five years... your friendship."

Her heart soared with his words. "You have no idea how much it means to hear you say that, Mal. From now on you're going to hear ever stupid little detail of my life," she said, nodding sagely.

"As if you didn't tell me every little thing already," Malcolm counted. "I recall often being told, and in great detail, nearly everything that went on with you. Especially during lady time."

She felt herself flush, her pale cheeks becoming reddened and warm. "You had to know, otherwise you'd have made a mess."

"A mess I wouldn't have minded at all," he said, his lips pulling into a sly smile. "Who knows, maybe I'll still make that mess."

"Oh boy," she said, feeling her heart race. "You cannot talk like that with the little one here."

His smile turned innocent as he nodded. "But once we get home and put her down in her new room, all bets on where this conversation will go are off."

"Be careful what you wish for," she said brazenly, hoping that he would act on his words. It bothered her somewhat that he was still conflicted about his feelings but every time she was, she told herself to be more understanding. It had been less than twenty four hours since coming back into his life, despite it feeling like a life time. It would take time and understanding, and perhaps a few feminine tricks to get what she wanted. "Let's go home."

Malcolm nodded and sat up in his seat as he repositioned the back to an upright position. "Wake up munchkin, you need to sit in the back," Malcolm gently said to his daughter.

She didn't stir from her slumber in her mother's arms, in fact, she turned over, burring herself into Elizabeth's chest even more.

"She's always like that," she said. "I've never been able to wake her up when she's out like this."

"Alright," he said softly, a smile lighting up his face. "Here, I'll take her and put her in the back."

Elizabeth nodded in agreement and helped him gently pick their daughter up. He stepped outside of the car with her and walked around to the backseat. From inside the car, Elizabeth could see that Malcolm had become distracted with something.

"Hold on a moment," he said as he opened up the backseat of the car. He set his phone down onto the seat and looked to Elizabeth for help. She turned around in her seat and helped her husband secure their daughter in the back. Even the cold had no effect on the young girl, as she was soundly snuggled up in the backseat, blissfully unaware of her surroundings.

"Alright, I'm back," Malcolm said into his phone. "Tell me that again?"

The color from his face drained as if he had seen a ghost. Anxiousness built up in Elizabeth's chest as she watched the strongest man she knew become deathly afraid. He stood out in the cold for a few moments longer, listening to the voice on the other end.

"Hey, Mal," she said gently. "Come inside, you'll get sick." She was trying to distract him, but her words didn't even reach him.

"You're sure about this?" he asked firmly. "Without a shadow of a doubt you are sure?" He released a deep sigh, the air freezing his breath as it escaped. "I'll tell them both you send your best, thank you for letting me know, Cameron." He hung up the phone and gently closed the back seat of the car. Instead of getting in right away, he paced outside for a few moments, visibly beginning to shiver.

Elizabeth wrinkled her nose as she stepped outside of the car and walked next to him. "Hey," she said soothingly. "What was that all about?"

Malcolm stopped moving around when she got close. He gazed her searchingly, as if he was looking to her for some answer that plagued him. "It was your brother calling to tell me what he found out about the information Brantford left behind for me."

Her body stiffened at the mention of her brother. "What was it?" she asked hesitantly. Though she was curious, the answer also frightened her.

"My father," Malcolm said slowly. "He's still alive."

Chapter Seventeen

Nothing would go right. Victoria was stuck in hellish traffic for over an hour. When Cameron finally drove close enough to see the cause of such a delay, she was upset to see that three cars had crashed into a construction site. Debris littered the roads and heavy machinery was tipped over onto the highway. The construction crew was able to clear the far left lane, leaving only that tiny area open for the huge amount of traffic coming through.

"Every year," she mutters to herself as. The annual first car accident, signifying the beginning of the winter, could not have come at a worse time. All Victoria wanted to do was be in a hot shower with food in her stomach.

"Think of it this way," Cameron said through a smile. "It's just a little bit more time with me."

Victoria was thankful that she wasn't stuck in this alone. She recalled a time she went to go visit her mother and was caught in the worst traffic jam in years, spending six hour trapped in one place on a hot summer day. "It does help that you're here. I would go mad if I was by myself. I can't stand traffic."

He chuckled at her words. "I think it's universal that no one can," he said lightly. "But it could be worse."

She nodded, slightly annoyed, yet grateful for his cheerful attitude. "Say that when you have shit all over you." Her body shuddered in disgust, her skin felt as if ants were crawling all over her.

"I understand the feeling," he said sympathetically. "There are stories I could tell you about being in the military and the conditions I had to be in for weeks on end."

Victoria felt pangs of regret passing through her. "I'm sorry, Cam," she said softly. "I don't mean to be crabby. I just want to be clean... I think I'm beginning to smell."

"No need to apologize," he said kindly. "All I was saying is that, I get it." His head turned to look at her and his lips formed a comforting smile. "Here, now that I know it's just a stupid accident I'll cheat a little."

She raised a brow in confusion. "Oh?"

He winked at her and reached across her body into the glove compartment. Inside was a blue light connected to a cord. Rolling down the window, he stuck the light on the roof of the car and plugged in the cord into the circular outlet on the dash. At once the front of the car was illuminated with a bright, spinning blue light. The cars in front of them parted like the red sea allowing them to pass. "See?" he asked through a grin. "Cheating."

Her lips pulled into a tight smile as the pace picked up considerably. "You're my hero," she said truthfully.

"To protect and serve," he said lightly. A chuckle escaped his lips as more and more cars parted to let them by.

"Be honest with me," Victoria suddenly said, her tone serious. "How are you? Don't joke or be as stoic as you normally are."

Cameron stiffened at the wheel, his hands gripping it so tight they became bone white. "I don't know," he admitted after a long silence. "I'm happy that everyone is safe. That my niece is back with her parents, that you and my sister are still alive. Hell, I'm happy that Malcolm won... but none of that changes the fact that I lost my brother."

She nodded sympathetically and reached over to gently place her hand on his. "I'm so sorry, Cam," she said softly. "Here I am going on about nonsense when…"

He cut her off with a wave of his hand. "It's not nonsense," he said in a shaky voice. "Frankly, I'd much rather hear about your problems than talk about mine. My brother's body died today, but he was gone a long time ago."

She didn't believe his words. His eyes told a different story; one of sadness and regret. It was difficult to fight her curious nature and stop herself from digging deeper. Out of respect for him, she bit her tongue and leaned back into her seat. "Well," she said after a moment. "I don't have any earthly idea how I'm going to get rid of this smell."

"Rub lemons on your skin," Cameron responded, his body relaxing slightly.

"That sounds naughty," she said, giggling slightly.

"You say that now, but really," he pressed. "Do it. The smell will disappear and make your skin look shiny and new."

Her lips pulled into a smile, and her hand gently squeezed his. "Thank you for the advice."

"I should be thanking you," he said with forced cheerfulness. "It'll be a really nice fantasy tonight."

Victoria couldn't help but blush and feel a rush of heat flowing through her. *Stop that,* she demanded silently. She couldn't help that Cameron was being so nice when she was so vulnerable and in some need of reassurance that she was desirable. It was a feeling she hated more than anything and it caused her upper lip to wrinkle in self-contempt. *I will not let what happened with Malcolm make me do something I will surely regret.*

Victoria turned on some music to avoid the awkwardness and after a few moments of the sound filling the car, she was able to relax. Thankfully, Cameron's slight abuse of power shortened the trip down to less than fifteen minutes, and once they arrived she eagerly exited the car.

"Do you want to come up?" she asked hopefully. *Why would you ask that? Get a grip, Victoria.* He shook his head, a soft smile on his lips. "I would like to but I need to run down a lead for Malcolm."

She was a bit disappointed, but she nodded in understanding. "If you need any help, just let me know." She didn't know why she offered to help him, perhaps to give Cameron some company or because it made her feel close to Malcolm. Either way, she thought she was being stupid.

"I will, but for right now you get some rest," he replied back, a genuine smile painted on his face. "You've earned it."

She smiled back at him. "Don't wait too long, I start at the tribune on Monday. Hopefully I won't have any time to worry about this anymore."

He chuckled. "I'll think about it. Now shoo, go rub yourself with lemons."

"Oh I will," she said, winking at him playfully. "Thanks for everything Cameron."

"Anytime."

She closed the door and stood there as he pulled the car away. It was difficult to watch him leave and then be left alone with her worries and doubts. Even the cold did little to distract her from the thoughts of Malcolm and Elizabeth becoming closer. *I made my choice,* she reminded herself. *I was protecting myself from more pain.*

Maybe Malcolm had been telling the truth, and the kiss was just something to provide them closure. But it was easier to believe that it was the start of something new for the two of them. A gust of chilled wind ripped at her face and brought her back to her senses. She ran inside the building, avoiding people as best as she could.

"I'm home," she said as she entered her apartment but hoping that Chloe was gone.

"Hey!" the redhead exclaimed from her room.

Victoria groaned, and quickly shuffled into the bathroom. "I'll be out in a few. I need to shower."

"Alright," Chloe replied back. "I have some news for you later."

"Can't wait," Victoria said, somewhat truthfully. She'd much rather hear about how her friend was doing than be left with her own dark thoughts.

Olivia Noble

Cameron's advice to use lemons was absolutely divine. The blood and the smell of it dissipated into nothingness almost as soon as the lovely acidic fruit touched the gore on her skin. After her shower, she felt refreshed, clean and like a brand new person. She would dispose of her clothes later, for now she just threw them into a trash bag along with the lemon she used to clean her skin.

"Is everything okay?" Chloe asked with a raised brow. She had been sitting on the couch, respectfully keeping her distance.

"As fine as it can be," Victoria replied. "So tell me your news."

Her friend gave her a skeptical look for a moment, as if debating on what she should say. "Well," she started slowly. "Dominic filled me in on everything."

Victoria whistled in surprise. "So what was the big secret?"

Chloe wrinkled her nose. "Everything, Vica. Don't go acting coy, too."

A guilty feeling welled up in Victoria's stomach. "I'm sorry, I just… it's all pretty fucked up, right?"

"I'd have appreciated being told about secret societies and my friend being put in mortal danger over some stupid fight between men and their giant cocks," Chloe said accusingly. "But I understand why you didn't tell me. It wasn't your place anyway, it was Dominic's and he has."

A small smile formed on Victoria's lips. She was glad her friend wasn't too angry with her. Chloe's wrath was the last thing Victoria needed to add onto her pile of crap right now. "So are the two of you okay?"

Chloe nodded happily and turned her hand over to expose a generously sized rock. "Yes! He asked me to marry him."

Once again, Victoria was shocked but thrilled at the same time. "Holy crap!" she exclaimed. "Chloe, that's great!"

"I thought maybe it would be good to have some kind of double wedding," Chloe said excitedly. "What do you think?"

"Maybe," Victoria replied, looking away to mask her pain. "But I doubt it."

"Oh no," Chloe said. "What happened?"

Victoria sighed and turned her back to her friend. "Nothing," she replied sadly. It hurt too much to talk about and she didn't want to drag down Chloe's good mood. "I'm going to make some food, I'm starving," she said, trying her best to sound cheerful.

"Alright, there is some lunch meat of mine

you can have. I know you haven't gotten a chance to go shopping since you came back," Chloe said sweetly.

Victoria was grateful to have Chloe as her best friend. The innocent young woman was always so generous with her food and in almost all aspects of her life. It made Victoria a better person and right now, she really needed that kindness. With shaky hands, she opened the fridge and grabbed what she needed to make herself something to eat. A loaf of bread, Dijon mustard, Swiss cheese slices and some left over honey roasted turkey.

She laid out four slices of bread for two sandwiches. Even though she didn't feel all that hungry, she knew that he body needed nourishment. First she put on the turkey and the cheese to one half of the bread, and opened up the glass bottle of mustard. She needed a knife to spread a thin layer over the two remaining slices, and went through the motions of picking one out of the kitchen drawer.

It was nice to be distracted by the mechanical aspect of making a sandwich. The task was just engaging enough to distract Victoria from her thoughts but simple enough that it wasn't frustrating. Good food was exactly what she needed right now to be okay after the events of the day. As soon as the delicious and powerful flavors of the sandwich mixed in her mouth, she knew that she would be right as rain.

A blunt and sudden pain brought her back to reality. She hadn't been paying attention to where she placed the butter knife on the plate as she completed her first sandwich. The heavy metal knife slipped off the plate and landed squarely on the top of her bare big toe. A grunt of pain escaped her lips and she looked down at the offending mental object.

"Such a fuck up, Victoria," she muttered to herself. She reached down to pick the knife up and tossed it into the sink. Now she needed another knife and felt like an idiot for wasting dishes. The dull, throbbing pain in her toe reminded her of her carelessness and re-enforced her irritation. *First you lose your man and now you're dropping shit all over the place.* Retrieving her second knife for the simple task of sandwich craft, she applied a more generous coating of mustard to remaining slice of bread.

She tossed the second knife into the sink in disgust as she walked away. Little mistakes drove her insane and she mentally berated herself for making more work for herself later. Walking back into the living room was an annoying task with her now injured toe. It hurt to put pressure on the area, and she favored her left side to avoid the pain.

"What happened?" Chloe asked with a raised brow.

"Something stupid," Victoria replied as she

lifted the sandwich to her lips. She took a large bite and swallowed quickly without hardly tasting the food. It irritated her that she had been looking forward to eating, but now she just wanted to get the motions over with.

"Stop being so grumpy and tell me what's wrong," Chloe said softly. "You can tell me anything."

Victoria stopped eating, setting her food down on the plate and leaning back against the comfortable sofa cushions. "I broke things off with Malcolm."

"What?! Why?" Chloe asked, nearly frantic. "I thought the two of you were going strong."

Sighing, Victoria threw her head back and looked up at the white ceiling of the apartment. "I saw him kissing his ex-wife at the Club," she finally said.

"I can't believe it," her friend said with righteous indignation. "That bastard."

"Don't say that, Chloe," Victoria responded nearly listless. "The two of them have had it really rough. That whole secret society and dueling nonsense Dominic filled you in on was what ripped them apart, unwillingly." Even as she tried to be objective and respectful of what she saw, it still pained her to voice it out loud. Malcolm was supposed to be hers, he promised her that he was.

"Still," Chloe huffed out. "He was with you. He made a commitment."

"He told me that he had chosen me, that the kiss was just the two of them closing the chapter on their feelings," Victoria said softly. She desperately wanted to believe those words, but what she saw frightened her. More than anything, she didn't want to get hurt again. The image of catching the two of them one day having sex was vivid in her mind, making her want to vomit up the little bit of food she had consumed.

"What are you going to do now?" Chloe asked, placing a gently hand on Victoria's back.

"I don't know," Victoria said softly, leaning back into her friends touch. Tears stung the back of her eyes as she said, "I really love him, you know. I hate myself for it, but I do."

"Don't say that, Vica," Chloe said soothingly. "He was really good up until now and from what Dominic told me, the two of you have been through a lot together in a short time. There is nothing wrong with how you feel."

The warm, salty droplets cascaded down Victoria's face. "But he loves her," she said weakly. "I know he does. I can see it in his eyes and the way they look at one another. I hate myself because I want him all for myself. I want to be selfish."

"Then maybe you should be," Chloe said gently. "You deserve to be selfish. You've always put everything ahead of yourself. Work, friends, school… everything; don't you think it's time you start putting yourself first?"

"I can't," Victoria said, shaking her head. "It's wrong."

"Vica," Chloe said compassionately. "I don't know what to say. I just want you to be happy."

"I am happy," Victoria said sincerely, her voice shaky and her breathing labored. "I have the best friend in the whole world."

"Then as best friend," Chloe demanded grandly. "I demand we have ice cream and watch some sappy romance until we've cried out all our tears!" she giggled lightly, her eyes becoming bright as she stood up.

"Thanks, Chloe," Victoria said, trying her best to feed off her friend's good mood. "But I don't want to do that. I want to focus on my new job this Monday and moving on. I don't need Malcolm to be happy."

Chloe grinned and nodded. "That's my girl," she said gently. "But are you sure you don't want ice cream? I just picked up some Cherry Garcia."

"Okay," Victoria said in mock defeat. "Maybe a couple of scoops."

"Yay!" Chloe said excitedly as she threw her arms around Victoria. "I'm always here for you, Vica. You're the best friend in the world, too."

"You're making me blush," Victoria said as more tears rolled down her face. She returned the embrace tightly, and buried her face into Chloe's flaming locks. "Alright. No more tears."

"Right," Chloe said, wiping away her own. "I'll be right back."

Feeling energized and better, Victoria was able to take a bite of her sandwich and actually enjoy the mixture of the flavors. Telling Chloe about what had happened was more cathartic than she expected, and was glad her friend pushed for the information.

"Hey, Vica," Chloe called out from the kitchen. "Your phone is ringing."

"Thanks," Victoria replied as she stood up. She walked into the kitchen where her purse was left sitting on the counter. Pulling her ringing phone from the outside pocket, she slid her thumb across the accept button and lifted the device to her ear. "Hello?"

"Yes, is this Miss Chase?" a stiff feminine voice asked over the phone.

"This is she," Victoria replied with a raised brow.

"I'm Margret from the Tribune, calling to tell you about the opening we had available for you," the woman said softly.

"Had for me?" Victoria asked, a sinking feeling forming in her stomach.

"Unfortunately," the woman said, hesitating only slightly. "The position has been closed. I'm sorry to tell you this."

"What do you mean it's been *closed*?" Victoria demanded. "Why?"

Olivia Noble

"I'm not at liberty to say," Margret said. "Good night, Miss Chase. I'm sorry it didn't work out."

The call ended before Victoria could say another word. In an instant her good energy transformed into a sinking pit of despair. "This is not happening," she said to herself in disbelief. She would call Malcolm and… she couldn't call Malcolm. She'd have cried more but she had no tears left to spare.

"Vica?" Chloe asked questioningly.

Victoria raised a hand. "I need to figure this out. I'm going to call Mr. White." She briskly turned around and walked toward her room as she furiously dialed her old boss' number. It rang for several long moments. "Don't you ignore me," she said in irritation.

"Hey, slugger," her boss said hesitantly. "I didn't think you'd be calling me after you landed the dream job."

"I just lost it, Mr. White," Victoria said, trying her best to keep her voice level. "Just ripped out from me in an instant."

He let out a long sigh before saying, "I know, kid. I was hoping you weren't calling about that."

"Mr. White, please tell me what's going on," she pleaded. "Can I come back?"

"Victoria, I hate to be the one to tell you this, but after the story you handed into me… I can't take you either."

"What?" she asked in confusion. "What the hell was wrong with my last story?"

"You failed to mention you were sleeping with him and biased about everything you wrote," he said harshly. "A competitor ran the story and now I'm up to my elbows in shit apologizing to the federal government."

"But they were wrong! Malcolm was innocent and I have proof of it," Victoria said, channeling her rage into every word. "Fuck what the gossip column has to say about me. I wrote the truth."

"Be that as it may, kid," he said sadly, "perception matters more than the truth. I'm sorry, Victoria, but you're never going to work in this town again."

"So that's it?" Victoria said, not able to comprehend what she just heard. "Years of busting my ass for you and getting you some really, really juicy stories and this is how you pay me back? One little bitch says I'm not reliable and suddenly I'm poison?" she was laughing hysterically now, it was just too ridiculous. "This is a joke, Cary," she said bitterly, dropping her respectful use of his last name. "It has to be."

"It's not," he shot back. "Good night, Victoria. I hope it works out for you down the road."

"Fuck you," she said as she jabbed her thumb onto the end button. Her legs didn't feel strong enough to hold up her weight any longer. She slumped back against the wall of her bedroom and slowly sank to the floor. Somehow, she knew Malcolm was involved in this. She couldn't think of another reason why her life would suddenly crumble in an instant.

Pissed off that I didn't fuck him, I bet, she thought angrily. *Trying to control me with my job again. Fuck him.* The more she thought about it however, the less it made sense. Malcolm had been kind to her when they left and he was too busy spending time with his family.

She had incorrectly thought she had no more tears to spare and that the worst had already happened.

Life proved her wrong.

Now she had lost everything and the only person she could turn to was the one person she was determined to let go of. "Dammit!" she screamed as tears gushed out of her eyes. "Dammit!"

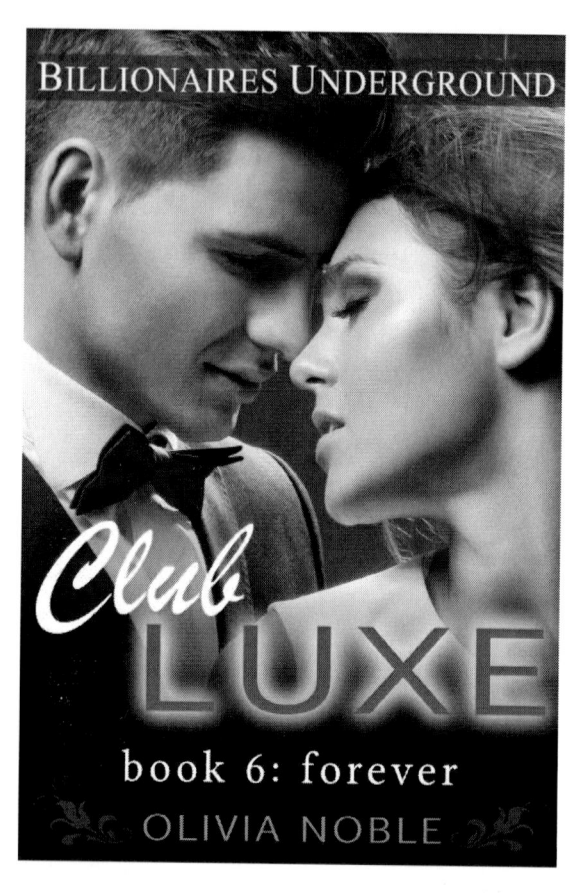

The stunning conclusion to the Club Luxe series is now available!

Club Luxe 6

Victoria has lost nearly everything she cared about. Her man and her job seemed to evaporate overnight and there isn't anything she can do about it. With Malcolm's history of blackmailing her into getting his way, she can't even be sure that he isn't the reason for all this.

Getting back his family should have made Malcolm the happiest man in the world. Yet, there was something critical missing: Victoria. Being away from her forced him to realize that she was the love of his life. Even though Elizabeth and Claire were in his life again, he knew that he had to do whatever it takes to get his woman back.

To receive a FREE book, sign up for Olivia's mailing list today:
eepurl.com/TRg95

Like on Facebook:
facebook.com/AuthorOliviaNoble

Email the author:
\

Made in United States
North Haven, CT
12 August 2025